DILEMMAS OF A DAMSEL

Part I

Monique Elise

ISBN: 1547224649
ISBN 13: 9781547224647

This book is dedicated to the loving memory of my beautiful Aunt -Robin Lowery. Continue to rest in peace...

ACKNOWLEDGMENTS

I would like to first express my sincerest gratitude to my readers. The fact that you have taken a genuine interest in my work is truly humbling and I thank each and every one of you! Honestly, I'm not sure I would've done this without the love, support, and encouragement from my friends and family. Thank you all so much for letting me talk your heads off about my ideas and helping me make this series be the best it could possibly be. And of course, without God none of this would be possible. Thank you for answering my prayers, and giving me the courage to not only take a chance on myself, but my art as well. This book is dedicated to all of you fabulous women out there! Be amazing... xoxo Monique Elise

PROLOGUE

It was an unbearably hot summer night. Michelle anxiously paces the living room, her skin sticky and nerves on edge. The cold air from the air conditioner does little to calm her. She carried on this way for the last hour or so; taking a few steps toward the kitchen before turning around to pace towards the front door. The only time she broke from this harrowing pattern was to check the time or take a peek out of the blinds facing the driveway. Each time she did, she felt more and more ridiculous and equally ticked off; her husband Cliff hadn't come home in two days.

Her angst was briefly interrupted by two small sets of feet scattering around upstairs. Jade and Aleena, her two young daughters, were supposed to be getting ready for bed. She didn't want to alarm them, but she sensed they were beginning to suspect something was wrong. After kissing the girls goodnight and tucking them in, Michelle returns to the kitchen and pours herself a much-needed glass of wine. Tilting her head back and closing her eyes, she indulges in the crisp taste and allows the plum aromas to tickle her nose. Once she reopens her eyes, she immediately picks up the phone and dials her husband's pager yet again. Now, all she could do was wait and hope that the phone would ring sooner rather than later. Determined to keep herself occupied, Michelle resigns to turning on some music and folding the laundry she'd been neglecting for the last few days.

Another hour has passed and still no word from Cliff; now she was starting to panic. The sultry voice of Sade fills the room but does little to mellow her out. Frustrated, she decides to pour herself another glass of wine. Michelle walks into the living room, and takes a seat on the couch. Extremely conflicted, she grabs a cigarette from pack on the coffee table, places it on her lips and lights it up. The tobacco fills her lungs and she eagerly embraces the sensation by sinking back into the couch and taking another long drag. Lost in the music and a cloud of smoke, she stares at the wall contemplating the right moment to call the police and file a missing persons report.

Two hours and a bottle of wine later, Michelle sees headlights creep into her driveway. Lifting herself up, she walks over to the window, glances out the blinds and sees her husband getting out of the car. A sense of relief initially washes over her, she was thankful that he was unharmed. But as he made his way towards the house, she became really angry. Ready to confront him, she takes a step back and positions her hands on her hips, preparing herself to either hear an apology or to square off. Cliff had quite the temper and never took too kindly to being questioned by his wife. Her heart raced as she could hear the jingle of his keys and sound of the door unlocking. Then, after two long days, she is finally face to face with her husband.

"Where have you been? I was worried sick!" Michelle says.

Without saying a word, Cliff walks right past her and heads straight for their bedroom. Astonished and refusing to back down, Michelle follows after him determined to air out all of her frustrations.

She hisses, "Don't you think you owe me some type of explanation? You've been gone for two days Cliff! The girls haven't stopped asking about you!"

Cliff proceeds to opening the wardrobe closet and grabs a large duffle bag. Michelle watches him in horror before grabbing his hands.

"Cliff! Talk to me, what are you doing?"

Michelle stares into her husband's eyes pleading. She searches for the man she fell in love with, the man she married and had two beautiful children with. But to her dismay, she couldn't find him; the man looking back at her was hard and cold as ice.

Cliff finally says, "I'm leaving you Michelle, I want a divorce."

Michelle's eyes grew big and bewildered, "What the hell are you talking about? You're just going to leave me and your kids?"

Michelle grips his wrists refusing to let him go. Annoyed, Cliff flings her thin arms off of him.

He says, "That's exactly what I'm doing; now get out of my damn way."

Without hesitation, he begins gathering his clothes and throwing them into the bag. Michelle stands there stunned; his words sting, causing her chest to feel heavy with anguish. She knew their relationship was not perfect and that things were rough lately, but she couldn't grasp what she was hearing. She gave up so much for this man, dropping out of college to become a housewife and support his dreams. Slaving day in and day out to be a mother to his *children and the wife that he claimed he wanted. The realization that all she had sacrificed for this marriage was no longer good enough made her skin hot with rage.*

"You piece of shit! I spent my life taking care of this family while you're gone for days doing God knows what. And now you have the damn nerve to tell me you don't want it anymore? What am I supposed to do Cliff?"

"Do whatever you have to do, but I'm done. I'm not in love with you anymore. She doesn't want to be alone and she shouldn't have to be."

Before she knows it, Michelle slaps Cliff across the face. Hot tears stream down her cheeks and she screams out in a fury. Unbeknownst to her, all the commotion woke up Jade and Aleena, who are now standing in the doorway bearing witness to their parents fight.

Without saying another word, Cliff zips up his duffle bag, kisses his crying daughters and walks out of the house, leaving his wife and children to pick up the pieces.

JADE

1

It's May 6th, and in less than twenty-four hours, nine to be exact, I will be twenty-nine. Twenty fucking nine! This is it; I officially have one year left in my beloved twenties. Part of me wants to be cheerful and say that time flies when you're having fun. But the other part is sweating with a slight panic; you know that subtle dread you feel when you think you've forgotten something? Let's see, Bachelor's Degree (check), MBA (check), paying off the student loans I took out to get those degrees (check), my dope ass apartment (check), amazing friends (check), exciting job (check), and of course my handsome cat Blu.

My phone goes off and I notice that it's on the other side of my 1400 square foot apartment. I hop out of bed and scramble to grab it before the ringing stops.

I answer breathlessly, "Hello?"

"Hello sunshine!" My younger, chipper sister yells through the phone.

"Hey Aleena," I say as I settle down onto my couch.

Although we're five years and almost two hundred miles apart, my sister and I have always been close. Aside from how tight we were, we couldn't be more different. Where I've been known for my lack of tolerance and stern approach like our father, Aleena was more nurturing and understanding much like our mother. She was always the voice of reason and more willing to give others the benefit of the doubt. I always joke with her and say that she's soft, but she is merely a loving person. And it's one of my favorite things about her. Nonetheless, Aleena is the yin to my yang.

We fall into our usual chitchat right away. Discussing everything from what we did the night before, to catching up on the latest gossip, and discussing our thoughts on some of our favorite T.V. shows like *Insecure* and *Game of Thrones*. Before I know it, almost an hour has passed and we're still on the phone. I pick up my IPad and mindlessly check my emails. Blair, my best friend, just forwarded me a pass for the art mixer she's being featured in later tonight. I check the clock again and realize that I would need to start getting ready soon. I was looking forward to having a night on the town and bringing in my birthday with my girlfriends.

Aleena interrupts my train of thought, "Someone is knocking on thirty! So, are you finally ready to find a good man and settle down?"

And just like that, the excitement of my upcoming birthday is shattered by the realization that I still don't have a man. I can no longer deny the fact that my invisible clock is just ticking away. While Aleena is happy to be a twenty-four-year-old newlywed, I'm the furthest thing from settling down; something she wastes no time reminding me about.

Lord knows that I'm in no mood to discuss my love life right now. Don't get me wrong, I've definitely played the field and I've never had a problem attracting a man. I just have yet to find the right one. You know the one with the right amount of charisma, good looks, sex appeal, success, manners, and money? (Just to name a few.) I consider myself a professional at this dating thing. So much so, people in my past life once labeled me as the ultimate female bachelor. Yes, once upon a time I feared the thought of commitment and taking guys too seriously. I was known for my ability to juggle a few men at once and avoiding getting caught up. Simply put, I had no interest in settling down with anyone; I solely wanted to be wined, dined and entertained. Thankfully, that phase in my life has long worn off in the last year or so. However, something I will say is that dating so many people has helped me with one thing: I know exactly what I don't want. And as soon as I see a red flag I bail, refusing to waste anymore of my precious time. This small fact is exactly why I dumped Brandon only a few nights ago.

Brandon was a great guy. He was good looking, well spoken, and such a sweetheart. The sex was great and we had a lot of fun. He pretty much checked out on almost everything on my "list". But after a couple months of dating he began showing up to my place unannounced, calling me nonstop, and last week he drunkenly professed his love for me. No-fucking-way, I had to end it right there. I mean, yes I do want that eventually, but he was moving entirely way too fast. Regardless of all of that, I refused to get into the juicy details with Aleena right now.

Instead, I resign to brush it off and say, "Aleena! Please don't start. Not today."

"Ok fine. You're my sister and I only want the best for you," she replies.

Her disappointment is amusing. I say, "I know and I love you for it. But I would prefer it if we didn't discuss my love life right now."

We end our conversation, saying our "I love yous" and hang up. When I put the phone down, I can't help but to put my head in my hands and rub my temples. I know Aleena meant no harm, and I know she genuinely wants the best for me; hell, I want the best for me. But her persistence was beginning to wear me out. The older I get and the longer I stay single, the more I'm forced to defend the latter. Constantly pressured to answer questions and face judgment for my inability to find a man, settle down, and have children. Truth is; I'm sick and tired of being looked at as a second-class citizen because of my relationship status. Does the fact that I worked my ass off through undergrad and graduate school mean nothing? I'm one of the youngest senior marketing consultants at my firm and I got there with my own blood, sweat and tears. So why is it that my success is suddenly negated because I'm single? I'm a modern woman that's capable of achieving stability, financial security, and happiness on my own. Why isn't that celebrated?

It's not like I'm not trying. Shit, you think I'm putting myself through these torturous love games to not find the one? I love a good fairytale ending just like the next girl, and I still have hope that my prince charming is out there. But I utterly refuse to settle until I find him. What's wrong with that? I look up and check the clock again, I had to hurry up and get to the mall if I wanted to have something to wear tonight. The last thing I want to do is make myself feel any worse. And there's nothing like forgetting my woes with a relaxing shower followed by retail therapy. I hop up and head straight for the bathroom.

The hot water from the shower is soothing as it cascades down my skin. I close my eyes and tilt my head back enjoying the sensation. Before I can stop them, the memories of my father leaving us invade my mind. Although he was a complete ass for abandoning us the way he did, part of me also blamed my mother. At my age, my mother was already married with two kids. I mean, yes she took care of her family, putting her dreams and aspirations aside for us, but in the process she completely forgot about her own self. I believe that was one of the worst mistakes she could've ever made. Really what's the point? You forget who you are for a man and then the moment he decides he's tired of you, you're left alone to pick up the pieces. Honestly, that's one of my biggest fears: settling for the wrong guy, losing myself, and ending up right where I started, alone. Even though my parents ended up reconciling after a few years and my father tried tirelessly to make up for his mistakes, I wasn't too thrilled about it. I would never forget watching my mother be in so much pain over a man; witnessing that still haunts me till this day. But honestly I don't know who is worse, him for leaving or her for taking him back.

Upon exiting the shower, I reach for a towel and wrap it around my damp body. I walk up to the vanity mirror and wipe away the fog from the steam. Leaning in, I take a deep breath and stare at the person looking back at me. One thing is for sure; the older I get, the more and more I'm beginning to resemble my mother. Dark brown almond shaped eyes, cognac skin, narrow nose, full lips, dark brown hair, and 5'8 slender frame. Please believe me when I say that I love my mother; however, I have absolutely no desire to be like her. Once in my bedroom, I check my phone and see a missed call from Blair. I call her back right away.

"Hey girl," Blair answers the phone with cheerfulness in her voice.

"Sorry I missed your call, I was in the shower. What's up?" I reply.

"You're still coming to the art show tonight right?" She inquires.

"Duh, I'm about to head downtown and get an outfit now. Where are we going afterwards?"

"There's this new spot Viper that I wanted to check out. It's supposed to be super nice."

"Cool!"

Blair suddenly asks, "So, are you bringing Brandon?"

"Girl," I begin as I reenter my bathroom, grab my favorite body lotion and rub it into my skin, "I had to cut that man off," I reveal.

"Jade! Why? I thought you guys were getting along great! What happened?" Blair asks.

Blair's disappointment is especially felt, because she, along with her boyfriend Jayson, are the ones responsible for setting Brandon and I up. Frankly, they were sick of me being a third-wheel on their dates and decided to step in. A chance run in with Jayson's old college buddy turned out to be the perfect opportunity to play cupid.

"He was trying to get too serious," I answer.

She says, "And what's wrong with that? I thought that was what you wanted? I love you Jade but you kill me."

Blair was a free spirit and she wasn't afraid to be brutally honest with me. Ever since our first day of high school, we've been inseparable. Back then, she was the new girl in town with an animated view of the world and I was the timid freshman that was ready for a fresh start. She was my best friend and I appreciated her kind heart; I loved that she always tried to see the good in people. I knew that like my sister Aleena, Blair only wanted the best for me. Nonetheless, Blair's badgering became exasperating. She just didn't understand; I want what I want and there's no in between.

And as if she was reading my mind, Blair lectures, "I swear Jade you're so damn picky! If you keep this shit up you're going to end up a lonely old lady living with your crazy ass cat."

I chuckle and look down at my adorable Pixie-bob cat Blu. He was comfortably seated at the foot of my bed taking a nap.

I retort, "I resent that statement."

"Well what do you want?" Blair says.

"Nothing that Brandon has to offer."

Blair doesn't hide her aggravation, but she decides to throw in the towel on the topic, "Ok whatever you say Jade! I'll see you tonight and don't be late!"

We hang up the phone and I dress quickly, eager to enjoy my weekend.

By the time I arrive at the art show, I'm ready to mingle, support my best friend's means for artistic expression, and have a good time. The area is open with large white walls and wooden mahogany floors. The ceilings are high with tall black pillars and long white pipes stretching across the room. Spectators are aligned among the space, admiring Philly's own unique artists and their eclectic pieces of work while sipping cocktails and engaging in friendly dialogue. I make my way through the crowd clutching my purse and glass of champagne in search of Blair. After a moment, I spot her and Jayson posing for a picture. Never one to disappoint, Blair looks astounding; her hair is wild and full of life, and her makeup is superb. You can't help but to be mesmerized by her silky chocolate skin. When she sees me, she instantly runs over and greets me with a warm hug.

"Thank you for coming!"

"I wouldn't miss it for the world," I say, hugging her back.

By the time we break our embrace, Jayson is standing next to us.

"What's up Jade," he nods.

"Jayson," I coolly reply.

It's not that I don't like Blair's boyfriend, I just don't like him for her. To be frank, I think he's a piece of shit. He is the prime example of why I choose to be picky (as Blair says). Although he puts up a good front of being the lovable, caring boyfriend; I can see right through it. Simply put, Jayson is full of crap and a master manipulator who, I'm almost certain, cheats on Blair. The vibes he gives off speaks volumes; it's something in those beady ass eyes. He looks at me and every other woman he encounters a little too long if you know what I mean. For the life of me I never understood how Blair fails to notice it. Hell! He's doing it right now, sipping his drink while his eyes are glued to another woman's ass. I clear my throat and he sees me watching him. Like I said, I love Blair for always seeing the good in people; however, I sometimes feel it gets her into trouble. But just like Blair can't force me be a kept woman, I can't force her to wake the hell up and dump her atrocious boyfriend.

I turn to Blair, "So where are your pieces girl?"

Without saying another word, she quickly leads me to her display. Blair is what I call an artistic chameleon. There's nothing she really can't do. When we were younger, she excelled as a pianist, in college she took up painting, and every once in a while she dabbles in poetry. She was popular amongst the art community and was often featured in plenty of showcases.

"Isn't this shit classy?" Blair says.

"Check you out!" I say high-fiving her. I take a moment to look around, "Where's Kara? I thought you said she was coming?"

Kara was another close friend of ours. After college, I met her at one of my first jobs. We started on the same day and have been close ever since. Naturally, Blair and Kara's relationship developed and blossomed as well. Kara had an infectious personality; she was silly as hell and a lot of fun. She was often the life of the party, and ready for pretty much anything. The two of us spent many nights running the streets together while Blair was cuddled up at home.

"She text me about an hour ago saying she wasn't feeling well and that she was going to stay home," Blair answers.

"That sucks! I'll be sure to check on her later."

Blair nods in agreement and we continue to chat. After a few moments and another drink, I suddenly feel someone staring at me. The little hairs on the back of my neck stand at attention as I quickly scan the room. I nervously take a sip of my champagne and then I see him. The chatter in the room quickly dissipates. Our eyes meet and it forces my heart to skip a beat. The attraction is instantly magnetic, so much so it almost causes me to choke on my beverage.

His eyes are so intense that I am too enticed to look away. His skin is dark cocoa that layered over his perfectly sculpted muscles; I could definitely tell that he worked out. He looked to be about 6'3 with a nice medium build; I guess he was a basketball player or a boxer. He has a little rough around the edges look to him, you know that look that most, if not all, women find to be intriguing. His bone structure is immaculate and he has a delectably strong jaw-bone. Whoever his barber was deserves an award because his Caesar haircut is sharp and complimented by a master-fully tapered beard. All the women in the room couldn't help but to be enthralled by his presence, myself included. I wondered how the hell I hadn't noticed him sooner because goodness he was sexy. He smiles revealing his pearly white teeth. I swear he put a spell on me, I was locked into place; the feeling was electrifying. Before I could return the favor, a small tap on my shoulder breaks me out of my trance. I turn around and come face to face with none other than Brandon. *Lord this is the last thing I need!*

Surprised, I give him a quick kiss on the cheek, "Brandon! I wasn't expecting to see you here."

"Blair invited me, she insisted I come," he replies.

I quickly shoot Blair, whom has conveniently made her way across the room, a venomous look. *Man I have some words for her!*

"Oh she did, did she?" I say.

"I really need to talk to you."

"About what?"

"About us Jade," Brandon says.

"Brandon, please don't do this here," I say before taking another sip of my champagne.

Damn I need another drink if I'm going to have to deal with him.

"What do you mean don't do this here? You won't return any of my calls Jade. What happened? I thought we were getting serious," Brandon pleads.

I sigh. The realization that this poor guy was going to make an awkward situation even more awkward makes me cringe. Refusing to cause a scene, I grab his hand and lead him outside for some privacy. He paces in front of me digging his hands into his front pockets.

"Look, what we had was fun. But you were taking things just way too serious for me and it kinda' freaked me out. You're a great guy, but I just want to be friends," I explain.

"Seriously Jade? What happened after three months? What changed?" He questions.

I look at him, struggling to find the right words.

Then I finally say, "You said you loved me while we were having sex."

"And what's wrong with that?"

"Then you cried."

He bows his head, shaking it in defeat. I stand there, uncomfortable; this was becoming painstakingly unpleasant.

"What do you want Jade?" He asks me, pleading.

"I'll know when I find it. I just know that whatever that is, isn't with you."

Shocked at my audacity, he peers into my eyes. He desperately searches for a glimmer of hope for some type of reconciliation; seeing none, his eyes turn cold.

"Fuck you," he says before turning and walking away. But about five steps in, he turns around and makes his way back over to me. He continues, "You know what? You think that 'cause you're cute and successful that you're hot shit, but you need to get off that fucking high horse and stop being so cold-hearted. You black women are all the same!"

Whoa!

"Excuse me? Where the hell did that come from?"

"You all complain about there not being enough good black men in the world. But when you find one, you treat him like shit! And then y'all wonder why we start dating white and Hispanic chicks. They don't give us half the drama y'all bitches do," he snarls.

As soon as the words leave his mouth, my free hand raises and swings across his face making contact. *SMACK!* Brandon grabs his cheek in disbelief.

I say, "I had no clue you were such an asshole! You can forget about being friends, and trust me when I say that those other women can have your corny ass."

"Have a nice life," he says before turning and walking away.

I gulp down the rest of my champagne and head back to the gathering. *I'm going to kill Blair!* I scan the room, ready to give her a piece of my mind. But to my dismay, she's nowhere to be found. I couldn't hide my annoyance, but I refuse to let Brandon ruin my night. The four hundred and fifty dollar pair of shoes I'm wearing had no time for that! I force myself to take a few deep breaths before walking over to the bar situated in the corner. This time I order a martini in hopes it will help to calm my nerves. I take two long sips and eventually feel my irritation and frustration pass.

I wander the rest of the party admiring the different works of art. The items on display are vast and beautiful. Everything from sculptures, paintings, and photographs filled the space, each having its own special appeal. Secretly I've always envied those that had the gift of artistic expression. I always felt that they had such a colorful way of looking at life as we know it. They were unafraid to be vulnerable and share themselves with the world; a far cry from just about all that I am: guarded, calculated, and meticulous.

By the end of the night I bump into a few friends, and make some new ones. As the crowd begins to evaporate, a small part of me is bummed because I was unable to locate Mr. Mysterious again. I have to admit I was anxious to cross paths. Then, a photograph immediately catches my attention and it's absolutely riveting. It was so simplistic yet equally intense. I stop and admire the imagery, captivated. It was a man and woman, naked, embracing one another. It was so raw. The way he held her, and she him, the two were intertwined like they were one. It was beautiful; this one photograph embodied all that I desired. I could feel a knot forming in my throat.

"You like this piece?"

His smooth voice startles me.

"Yes, it's stunning," I say, turning to see my mystery man, up close and personal.

I feel my heart catapult into a 5k race.

"Well thank you. I'm glad you like it," he smiles revealing his dimples.

"Wait, you took this?" My cheeks flush.

He playfully puts his hands up in the air and says, "Guilty as charged."

"Oh my, you're very talented!" I say, a little too excited.

We stand there in silence for a moment. Standing next to him, I get a whiff of his Bleu De Chanel cologne and my head spins.

"I'm Maxwell but you can call me Max," he says with his arm extended.

I was determined to keep it cool, "Jade." We shake hands and my goodness his hands are soft, "Nice to meet you."

"The pleasure is all mine Jade."

We engage in a bit more small talk before my cell goes off. I fish it out of my purse in a hurry with every intention of hitting ignore. Confusion rushes over me when I see Blair's name across the screen. Looking at Max, I excuse myself and walk a few feet away for some privacy. With Blair, you never know what it could be.

"Blair, why are you calling me? You're still here right?"

I can hear her hesitation through the phone. *Oh this can't be good.*

She begins, "Jayson isn't feeling well so we're going to head home. Please don't be mad!"

My face sinks, "Blair! We had plans! It's almost my birthday and we always bring in our birthdays together!"

I turn and see Max watching me with concern and I'm sure he thinks I'm crazy.

Blair says, "I know I'm sorry, but you understand. Plus we still have all day tomorrow to celebrate. Trust me I'll make it up to you!"

I roll my eyes. "Yea, you better," I snort.

"I love you!"

"Yea, yea," I say before hanging up the phone.

I walk back over to Max and he can see the annoyance written all over my face. Tonight was really turning out to be a complete bust.

"Is everything alright?" Max asks.

"Yes sorry about that. It was just my friend."

"Anything I can help with?"

I shake my head, "I don't want to hold you up."

"Trust me; I'm exactly where I want to be."

His forwardness is a turn on. Once again I can feel myself blushing against my better judgment.

"Well, I was supposed to be going out with my best friend for my birthday. But her boyfriend got sick and she had to go home," I say.

"I'd love to celebrate your birthday with you," he replies.

"Are you sure? What about the show?"

He chuckles, "Look around, it's practically over."

I cross my arms and assess the room, besides the two of us, there weren't many people left. A few folks had large industrial sized brooms and began sweeping debris from the floor.

I hesitate, tempted by his offer, "Sure, where to?"

It's the perfect spring night, the moon is high and the stars glistened. There's a slight breeze that causes my skirt to dance as I walk side by side with Max. Besides the chaos I was subjected to earlier in the evening, I'm happy that I decided to step out. I check my watch and see that it's twenty minutes until midnight, only a couple minutes away from my birthday.

We decided to take a walk to one of my favorite restaurants in the area. On our way there, we instantly vibe; getting to know one another and conversing like we're old friends. We discuss everything, from our embarrassing moments in high school, to memories of our first kiss, politics, and pop culture.

"So why did you choose to become an artist?" I ask.

"Because, art is in all things," he replies with confidence.

"Hmm, that's a good answer," I say, intrigued by his perspective on things.

"Why did you choose to become a marketing consultant?"

"It was all a part of my plan. I always liked helping people and solving problems, it kind of made sense."

Max nods with intent, "Do you enjoy it?"

"Yes, very much; I'm very excited about the work that I do and where my career is headed. I always saw myself being successful and independent. Luckily I found something I love that enables me to do so," I explain.

Once we arrive at our destination, Max stops ahead of me holding the door open. I smile at him as I walk inside. North Third was a hip and quaint spot in the Northern Liberties part of Philadelphia. It also happened to be one of my favorite spots to grab drinks; their blood orange margaritas were to die for. It was a Saturday night and the bar was packed with its usual crowd.

The hostess greets us with a smile; her hair was big and commanded your attention. She welcomes us and asks, "Table for two?"

I return the smile, "Yes please."

Grabbing two menus, she leads us to the back of the restaurant towards a dimly lit and intimate corner. We take our seats and she places the menus down.

"Someone will be right over to serve you," she says before turning and walking away.

Once Max and I settle in, I begin eyeing the menu eager to grab a bite to eat. I failed to realize how hungry I actually was. When I look up, I catch him watching me.

"What?" I ask.

"You are gorgeous," he says.

Max was very calm and certain about every word he said. It was intriguing as much as it was intimidating. I wasn't used to dealing with men that were absolutely secure and certain about themselves or what they allowed themselves to say.

My face flushes, giving away my nervousness. I smile and say, "Thank you."

"My pleasure," he responds.

Then, the waiter comes to our table requesting our order for drinks and slips back into the restaurant.

"So when did you become a photographer?" I ask, eager to take the attention off of myself.

"I got into it in high school. Actually, I dip and dabble in a few different things. I just have a lot to express and I'm able to communicate that through my art. Whether it's a picture, a painting or drawing," he explains.

I listen, mesmerized. *Shit, this guy is something else.* For some reason, he makes me anxious; it's a strange yet exciting feeling. As the night progresses, Max tells me about his love for art and some of his favorite things he's done throughout his career. By the time he's finished the waiter returns with our drinks and we order our food. We continue our conversation, discussing our upbringing and other interests before my phone goes off, indicating a new text.

Kara: HAPPY BIRTHDAY BEAUTIFUL!

I smile and quickly type a response.

Jade: THANKS LOVE! HOPE YOU FEEL BETTER. I'D LOVE TO SEE YOU TOMORROW!

I can feel Max's eyes on me again, causing my stomach to flip.

"Sorry, that was my friend," I say as I put my phone down.

Not a second later, my phone rings again, this time it's my sister calling.

"Hey Aleena," I say answering the phone.

"Happy birthday sis! Sorry I can't be there to celebrate with you but we can as soon as I'm back in town!" Aleena says with excitement.

"Thanks love!" I pause looking at Max, "Umm I'm kind of busy right now, can I call you back?"

"Busy? Jade it's midnight, if you're saying you're busy, that means you're up to no good!"

"Aleena, I will talk to you later. Love you."

She giggles, "Love you too hooch, use a condom."

My cheeks turn red as I hang up the phone and put it on silent.

"Sorry, that was my sister," I explain.

"No worries," Max replies with a smile.

He grabs his drink and I grab mine.

"Happy birthday Jade," Max says and raises his glass of gin.

I smile and follow his actions raising my margarita. Then we tap our glasses together making a toast to the night.

2

I wake up Monday morning and it's back to reality. I feel refreshed and ready to tackle my week. My weekend was an absolute whirlwind and I loved it. At work, I glide through the halls saying hello to my colleagues while sporting a chic ivory dress, paired with a new Chloe bag (a birthday treat to myself) and a kick ass glow. After I enter my office, I place my latte down on my desk before taking a seat and powering up my laptop. As it loads, I check my calendar and lay out my plan of action for the week. I have an important meeting to prepare for and a report I need to finish.

A soft knock on my door draws my attention. I look up and am greeted by my suit wearing, silver-haired boss Paul, "Good Morning Jade!"

Paul and I had a great working relationship; he valued my drive and ambition while I admired his wisdom and experience. Since joining the company three years ago,

Paul has always been supportive in helping me grow in my career and I respected him as my mentor.

"Morning Paul," I beam.

He casually takes a seat, "You look like you had a great weekend."

Paul knew that I celebrated my birthday this past weekend. In fact, last Friday he had his secretary organize a company happy hour in my honor. That's one of the many reasons I loved my job, they always found an excuse to party and make working with them fun.

"I really did."

He smiles, "I'm glad to hear that. I just wanted to make sure you had everything you needed and that we were all squared away with the McNair account for this afternoon."

I nod, "I have it all under control."

Paul seems pleased. He stands up to exit and says, "Never doubted you for a second. I'm free all morning so if you need anything just stop by my office."

"Will do."

Once he leaves, I dive right into my work. An hour or so has passed and I've managed to address my inbox full of emails that accumulated over the weekend. I just started putting the final touches on the presentation I would be briefing this afternoon before my cell goes off. I reach for my bag, pull it out of my desk drawer and retrieve my phone.

Max: I WOULD LOVE TO SEE YOU AGAIN. DINNER TONIGHT?

I smile at the thought, dinner sounded quite well to me. I hadn't stopped thinking about him and our chance encounter since we parted ways the other night. Not even a full-blown birthday celebration consisting of brunch, bottomless mimosas, and a few day parties with my girls could distract me long enough. Blair and Kara couldn't help but notice my demeanor; I was definitely smitten. They refused to let up with the questions. Stubborn by nature, I opted to keep my night a secret for a little while longer. I felt it was only right to guilt trip them for leaving me hanging. Hell, if it wasn't for them I wouldn't have had such a great evening; but they didn't need to know that just yet.

To be honest, I knew I wanted to sleep with Max a few minutes into our first date. So much so, I did the classic fidgeting with my keys and inviting him over for a nightcap when we left dinner. But to my surprise, he declined, opting instead to take my number, kiss me goodnight and go on about his business. That shit made me want him even more. Usually, I'm never this pressed on any guy. I mean, I know how to keep it together and test the waters before I decide if I really like him or not (let alone sleep with him). But this is hauntingly different. Getting a text from him was a pleasant surprise and I was definitely eager and willing to hang out with him some more.

Jade: TELL ME WHERE AND I'LL BE THERE...
Max: BET. I HAVE SOME WORK I NEED TO FINISH UP TODAY BUT I WILL

**LET YOU KNOW THE TIME AND
PLACE LATER ON.
Jade: SOUNDS LIKE A PLAN TO ME.**

I quickly type back before hitting send and putting my phone away. Feelings of elation rush over me and I feel like a young schoolgirl. The beginning stages of dating are always the most fun, intoxicating even. There is something about meeting someone new that gives me a boost of adrenaline. It's the excitement, the hope, and the endless possibilities. I long suspected that was the reason why I kept dumping guys without a second thought. Once done, I'm always eager to find a new match; I was addicted to the thrill of it. But as excited as I was, I was determined to get everything I needed to get done at work. With a deadline looming over my head, I couldn't afford to waste any more time.

It felt like the hours dragged at work today. I completed everything I needed to get done; my meeting went great and I even got a head start on some future commitments. But for some reason, I still felt angst; I couldn't shake the feeling. By five o'clock I was itching to get off and go home. True to form, I stop by the gym and perform my usual routine: thirty minutes of cardio and thirty minutes of light weight training.

Six thirty.
After I get home I do some cleaning: washing the dishes, wiping down all my glass top tables, watering my plants and sweeping the floor.

Seven thirty.
Finally, I tear off my clothes and take a nice hot shower, but even after all of that I'm still anxious. *What was taking him so long to get back to me?* Still damp and annoyed with my own desperation, I dry off, moisturize and put on my favorite vintage kimono robe. *I absolutely must relax!* Determined to do so, I walk into the kitchen and pour myself a glass of Pinot Grigio.

Eight o'clock.
After taking a long sip, I tilt my head back, close my eyes and relentlessly try to calm my nerves. (A habit I picked up from my mother.) But as the minutes continue to slowly pass by, I feel myself beginning to freak out. *Oh goodness what if he changed his mind?*

Before I know it, I'm simultaneously sipping and nervously pacing the house. Blu watches me with amusement, and he should, because I'm sure I look silly as hell. Then, when I was about to give up all hope, my phone rings, and it is bliss to my ears. I race back into my bedroom to retrieve it off my bed and quickly answer.

"Hello?" I answer breathlessly.

"I'm so sick of Jayson!"

"Blair? What are you talking about?" I say.

The last thing I wanted to deal with was Blair and Jayson's shenanigans. I always try to steer clear of their relationship drama. Tonight was no different.

"He's a piece of shit that's what!"

I sigh, "What happened?"

"He stayed out all night and didn't come home until this morning. Then, when I confront him about it he flips it on me saying I'm suffocating him."

I shake my head and go back into the kitchen to pour myself another glass of wine. I'm sure I will need it in order to listen to this. I don't want to be that friend that always talks shit about her best friend's boyfriend, but Jayson just makes the opportunity to do so far too easy. I never understood or expected for him to be in the picture this long. Because not only is he a certified creep, he's just as equally awkward. Let's put it like this: Jayson is no Max. He's just not smooth. It's pretty obvious that Max never had any issues with the ladies. That absolutely is not the case when it comes to Jayson; he was one of those late-bloomers. You know the kind of guy that got zero play from girls growing up because he had no swag? Well Jayson definitely came a long way, I'll give him that; but the newfound attention has had a huge effect on his ego. So the fact that he is always getting caught up is no surprise. Regardless, I can't understand for the life of me why or how Blair is even attracted to him because she could do so much better.

She continues, "I mean I wasn't suffocating when I was taking care of his sick ass now was I? I swear I'm so tired of this shit. He doesn't appreciate the type of woman he has and he'd rather run the fucking streets!"

"I know girl, but we've been through this. Nothing is going to change until you put your foot down."

"Yea I know," she responds.

The moment she utters those words, I know she isn't serious about making Jayson answer for any of his wrongs. But before I can try to convince her that she's worth more than her asshole boyfriend, another call comes through. I pull the phone away from my ear and see Max's name light up across my screen.

"Blair, I gotta go. I'll call you later ok?"

Before she can answer, I hang up clicking over to my other line.

"Hello?"

He says, "Hey beautiful. Do you think you can meet me in an hour?"

"Sure, where though?"

"My place," Max replies.

We hang up and I dress in a hurry, yearning to be in his presence yet again.

About an hour later, I'm stepping off the elevator onto his floor and walking towards his apartment. My Louboutin stilettos echo as they click down the long hallway. As I get closer, I can hear music in the background. Once at his door, I knock and a few moments later he opens up, looking even better than the last time I saw him. He grins showing off his billion dollar smile, steps aside, and lets me in. I walk inside and am instantly in awe of his place. It was all so open, yet super intimate. It was so him: intense, comforting and sexy.

"Wow, your place is amazing," I compliment.

"Thank you," he says.

It was a loft apartment with large windows overlooking the city, dark hardwood floors, and high ceilings. He had a living room set up with a fireplace, a spiral staircase in the corner leading up to his bedroom and elegant dining area. The soft voice of Jhene' Aiko fills the room and sets the mood. Bold pieces of art were strategically placed throughout the space and I can tell they were his work.

I turn to him impressed, "You're very gifted Max, you have a wonderful eye."

He meets my gaze, "I'm glad you think so."

"I do. I have to admit I've always secretly envied artists."

Max is intrigued, "Why?"

I shrug, "You're all so gifted; it's like you're looking at the world through a different lens. Like my best friend Blair, the way she is able to visualize and communicate feelings and messages through her craft is so phenomenal. Deep down I wish I could do that."

"Who says you can't?"

I quickly shake my head, "That is so not in my DNA."

He grins and approaches me, "From what I can tell you seem to be pretty amazing just the way you are."

Max then leads me into the dining area where there are place settings for two. He has me take a seat and I look around highly impressed. He returns with two plates of food and sets them down. Lamb lollipops, grilled asparagus and sautéed potatoes are on the menu tonight. The herbs and spices give way to a blissful aromatic experience, causing my stomach to dance with anticipation. He strikes a match and hovers over the table to light the single candle placed in the center. Then he takes a seat across from me, grabbing the place napkin and laying it onto his lap. I mimic his movements, doing the same. We both pick up our forks and knives before digging in.

"That was delicious," I say swallowing the last of my meal.

"Thank you," he smiles before wiping his mouth.

I reach for my glass and sip my pricey wine, "So is there anything you can't do?"

We giggle.

"I can't swim," he admits.

"Ha! I can definitely live with that," I answer.

"What about you?"

"Well," I pause, playfully stroking my chin, "I'm not the best dancer."

We laugh again.

I chuckle, "Yea I just keep it cute and basic with my two-step."

He laughs before finishing off his drink, "I have a hard time believing you can't dance. You're body movements are so fluid."

I quickly shake my head, "Looks can be deceiving."

"Prove it."

I almost choke on my drink, "What?"

He smirks, gets out of his seat and walks over to me. I watch him with curiosity in my eyes. Without saying a word he reaches his hand out, inviting me to take it. Blushing, I shake my head no once more.

"I don't bite."

"But I do," I challenge him.

His eyes light up with amusement but he continues to patiently wait for me to take his hand. Finally, I give in and choose to oblige him, allowing him to lead me into the living room. Lost in the music, our bodies become one. I let him lead me in a slow seductive dance. The electricity between us was hard to ignore. I look into his eyes and want to melt, I couldn't disregard the way he made me feel and I barely knew him. Consciously, I nibble on my bottom lip and he places his hand on the small of my back, pulling me in closer.

Before I know it, Max weaves his fingers through my hair and draws me in for a kiss. His lips were so soft and his kiss was so passionate. I welcome him into my space and match his pursuit. For a moment we are lost, consumed in one another's embrace. We let our bodies sway as our tongues wrestle provocatively. We make our way to his bedroom, the music is still playing and the mood is erotic. Once again, he's on me, it's as if he's addicted to my lips. He kisses me deeply before leading me to the bed and lying me down on top of him. I straddle him while his hands explore my body, rubbing my butt through my skin-tight jeans.

I place my hands on his chest and feel his defined pecs through his shirt. Flipping me over, he gently lays me onto my back and takes control. He peels off my clothes and then removes his. Max had the perfectly sculpted body of a God; everything about him was so alluring. I watch him with desire, anxious to feel him inside of me. Tracing his tongue down the length of my body, Max teases my nipples and causing them to grow harder with each touch. He climbs back on top of me and I wrap my legs around him as I throw my hands around his neck, sensually embracing all of him. He reaches into his nightstand and pulls out a condom before slowly sliding it on and entering me.

The weekend has returned and I'm ready for it. Between work, and spending all of my free time with Max, I was happy to be able to sleep in for a few extra hours. By the time I finally roll out of bed, it's noon. Aleena was treating me to a spa date and would be in town at any moment. I quickly hop in the shower and then dress for the day, putting on my favorite oversized T-shirt, leggings and running shoes. I throw my unruly hair into a loose bun and grab my stylish Gucci shades.

My phone goes off and I promptly answer, "Hello?"

Aleena says, "Hey sis. I'm downstairs, bring that ass."

I laugh at her silliness, "Be right down."

We arrive at the posh spa and are greeted by a warm receptionist. She checks us in and leads us into the changing area. Aleena and I get undressed, replacing our clothing with luxurious white cotton robes. We take a seat in the waiting area and sip our complimentary mimosas as we wait for our service to begin.

I say, "Thank you again for this Aleena."

"You're welcome, it's the least I could do for you," she replies.

"So how's married life treating you?"

"It's great! I really love it. Nothing is really different you know."

Aleena and her husband Nate were high-school sweethearts. Although I love Nate and I'm happy that he's my brother-in-law, I can't help but worry that Aleena is in over her head. I guess you can say that their seemingly perfect relationship is my Achilles heel. Like them, I too had a high-school sweetheart. I was Aleena, young, and hopelessly in love. Back then, I had my entire life figured out; but unlike my sister, my hopes and dreams were short lived.

My phone goes off and it's a text from Max.

Max: I CAN'T WAIT TO SEE YOU AGAIN.

I read his sweet message and can't stop the smile that takes over my face.

Aleena instantly takes notice, "Whose got you all giddy and stuff?"

I quickly text him back before putting my phone down, "This guy I met named Max." I sigh, "He is something else girl."

She can't hide her excitement, "How so?"

I explain, "Everything about him, everything is so right."

Suddenly, our masseuses enter the room and lead us back for our massages. After our spa date and a late lunch, I return home feeling serene and rejuvenated. I step off the elevator on my floor and walk towards my apartment. I can't wait to peel off my clothes and crawl back into bed. Once I reach my place, a bouquet of white roses meets me at my front door. Awestruck, I pick them up and read the small card attached.

> *Jade,*
> *I hope that you find these as beautiful as I find you...*
>
> *-Max*

I can't stop the butterflies from going rampant in my stomach. I can feel my face growing numb from smiling so hard. This has been one of the best weeks of my life.

3

A few weeks have passed and Max and I are riding with the windows down cruising through South Philly. The day is so beautiful; you'd be a fool if you weren't out enjoying it. The sun is high and bright, people migrated outside anxious to catch its rays. Children are in bliss; school is out. They finally had the chance to play games and run around with the pleasant smell of barbeque and summer lingering in the air.

"What's this we're going to again?" Max asks, interrupting my thoughts.

He glances at me looking as good as ever. Flashbacks of our morning lovemaking run through my mind. I cross my legs in an attempt to control my never-ending desire for him.

"Jade," he softly takes my hand.

"Huh?"

He grins and repeats his question, "What are we going to?"

I instantly sit up and turn to him, stunned, "You've never been to a night-market before?"

He shakes his head.

"Wow. I'm shocked!"

He raises his eyebrow, "Why?"

"I don't know, you seem so hip to everything."

Max doesn't hide his amusement, "I do?"

"Yes, but don't get me wrong I'm more than happy to show you a thing or two," I flirt.

This time, we both laugh before falling back into a comfortable silence; something I have grown to appreciate. There's something to be said about being so content with someone that you don't need to have mindless conversations for the sake of only having them. Being around Max was as easy as breathing; he was a no bullshit type of guy, very much like my father. Surprisingly, I found it to be quite refreshing and attractive. With him, he was straight to the point. There's no games, something I've sadly become used to dealing with over the years. As we near our destination, I feel myself get nervous. This is the first time Max will be meeting my friends.

"What's wrong?"

I smile and lie, "Oh nothing."

"You sure?"

I nod my head yes, "So, are you ready to meet my friends?"

"Of course I am. Who exactly is going to be there?"

"Well, my best friends Kara, Blair and Blair's boyfriend Jayson," I say with a hint of annoyance in my voice.

"You don't like him much huh?" He chuckles.

"Is it that obvious?"

Max nods his head as he smoothly parks his Mercedes. I watch him as he gets out, comes to my side, opens the door and helps me out of the car.

I explain, "Sorry, he just rubs me the wrong way."

"It's cool babe," He says before taking my hand and kissing it once more.

We walk towards the South Philly Night-Market hand in hand. Every year, various food vendors set up shop in different parts of the city with their best menu items in tow. Food enthusiasts like myself come from all over to indulge in local favorites and discover new ones. As we get closer the crowd thickens, I can see the streets filled with diverse food trucks and eager foodies. I spot a Korean BBQ truck and instantly pull Max in that direction, I've waited months for this.

While waiting for our food, a trio of loud and obnoxious females head right in our direction. Once they spot us, they quickly quiet down and get in line. I can't help but to giggle at them and the way they were gawking at Max. I get it; he's a tall fine glass of chocolate milk. I mean he does look exceptionally good. The way he could rock a simple T-shirt with jeans and make it look like a million bucks never ceases to amaze me. Since meeting Max, I've grown used to the envious stares I've received from other women. But he paid them absolutely no mind; he was all about me and I loved it. This time was no different. The ringleader of the pack had a bad dye job and her clothes were a size too small. Our eyes meet and she gives me a phony smile. I can sense that she was bold enough to try and get Max's attention in front of me. I decide to challenge her by smiling and saying hello. But before she can reply, I hear my name being called in another direction.

I turn to see Blair, Kara and Jayson making their way over to us. They already have some food in their hands. We greet each other and I can tell they are eager for an introduction. Max is as cool as ever when he introduces himself. I can see Kara and Blair are excited to finally meet my mystery man. They can't help but to eye him like he's a shiny new toy.

After we get our food, I say, "Let's find somewhere to sit I'm starving."

We walk a few feet and find a free bench in the neighborhood park. Children are playing while their parents watch and eat.

"Aye, Max...who are you riding with in the finals man?" Jayson asks.

"OKC," Max responds.

Jayson counters, "Nah man, Cleveland all day."

The two of them get lost in their conversation about the NBA and who they think will come out as this year's champs. I never understood how guys that don't know a thing about one another can instantly bond over a sports game. Amused, I continue to watch them as they walk away to get us all drinks. I pick up my shredded beef taco and place it in my mouth. As I take another bite and savor the amazing flavors, I can feel two sets of eyes watching my every move.

I pause, "What?"

Kara and Blair can't hide their excitement. The fact that I brought someone around the group was a luxury they were rarely afforded. They didn't waste any time fishing for details.

"Well, you two seem to be getting along great," Blair says with a nod of approval.

Kara's doe eyes light up with excitement. "Oh my God! Is he the artist guy? He is so fine!" she whispers.

"Guys relax!" I order, continuing to eat my food. "So where is Rashad? I thought he was coming?" I ask Kara, desperate to change the subject.

"Well he was supposed to come, but…"

"Here we go," Blair murmurs.

"He had to work," Kara answers.

She desperately tries to avoid my now prying eyes. Kara was a hopeless romantic that loved the idea of getting swept off of her feet. For some reason, she was always attracted to guys that had no interest in giving her what she wanted. Much like me, Kara never had issues getting a man. They often found her baby face, caramel skin and petite figure hard to resist. Nonetheless, she never quite succeeded in meeting one that had good intentions. After a few moments, she finally meets my gaze.

"Still with the bullshit huh?" I assume.

Kara nods, embarrassed. "I don't get it, things will be going so good and then he finds a reason to disappear," she shrugs, clearly defeated by the situation.

I ask, "Kara why do you keep doing this to yourself?"

"I don't know. It's completely different with him, we connect on a different level," she replies.

"Yea till he gets tired of you," Blair says.

Kara continues, "I mean it's not like I'm sitting at home waiting for Rashad to come around. Shit I do me."

"If you say so, Kara; Rashad does this time and time again because you allow him to," Blair accuses.

Oh the irony.

By now, Kara is completely fed up and rightfully so. Blair could be relentless with her judgment at times. But it was a bit ridiculous being that she rarely ever took her own advice.

"Blair, how about you worry about your man and I'll worry about mine!" Kara scolds.

Blair refuses to back down, "My man and I are just fine thank you."

Kara rolls her eyes, "Yea, this week."

Before I can attempt to step in and interject, the guys return with our drinks. Max takes a seat next to me and begins to dig into his chicken teriyaki.

"So Max, how long have you been a photographer?" Kara, who is back to her chipper self, wastes no time hitting him with the interrogation.

"I got into it in high school. I was in and out of trouble and my mom made me use my time more effectively. I guess it's helped me keep my head on straight," he says.

We all listen intrigued; I never heard this story. I mean I knew he got into art while he was in high school, but I didn't know the reason behind it. Before I know it, Blair joins in and she and Kara are relentless in getting to know Max better.

"Do you have any kids?"

"Have you ever been married?"

"Do you have any single brothers?"

Alright, enough is enough.

I refused to allow my friends to embarrass me any further, "Ok y'all damn! This isn't a job interview!"

We all burst out laughing. Max takes my hand, weaves his fingers in mine, and squeezes to show his appreciation.

"Well, I don't know about y'all but I'm ready for some dessert," Jayson says in an attempt to divert Blair and Kara's attention.

Blair claps with excitement, "Yes! I have been looking forward to getting some beignets!"

We finish our food and wander the night market excited to check out more vendors and sample unique treats and drinks. A live band is playing their best rendition of Prince's "Little Red Corvette." Before we know it, the sun is beginning to set and I feel as if I am going to pass out from a food coma.

Suddenly, I hear Jayson say, "Yo! Brandon! What's up man!"

Kara whispers, "What the fuck?"

To my horror, I see Brandon, the man I slapped a few weeks ago, in the flesh. The two eagerly greet each other with a handshake and quick hug. We make eye contact and I cringe; he looks at me as if I'm the she-devil herself. I glance at Max and instantly want to leave.

Brandon smiles, "What's up ladies?"

I can smell the tequila hanging on his breath. Kara smiles and waves but stays silent; I can tell that she's just as uncomfortable as I am. She and Blair were more than aware of our last encounter.

"Hey Brandon, I didn't know you hung out in this part of town," Blair says in an attempt to break the ice.

"Yea I'm here with some friends," he explains while staring at me, "What's up Jade."

"Hi."

Brandon notices me holding Max's hand and smiles.

"You're not going to introduce me to your friend?"

His words were a bit slurred, his eyes are glossy and he's wobbly on his feet. I knew that he wanted to start trouble, but I refuse to let Brandon get a reaction out of me. Not now, not today.

I turn and look at Max, "Max this is Brandon, Brandon this is Max."

"Sup' man," Brandon says to Max and reaches for a handshake.

The two quickly shake hands and I take a sip of my frozen margarita. A few moments later, two other guys join us and they are just as drunk as Brandon. He introduces us all and I can feel his friends eyeing me with amusement. I can't help but wonder what Brandon has told them about me. Small knots start to form in my stomach causing it to cramp with anxiety. Luckily, the trio gets distracted by another friend that joins them.

Max notices my demeanor and softly asks, "You ready to go?"

I quickly nod my head yes and squeeze his hand.

I turn to my friends, "Alright guys! We're going to head out."

I try everything in my power to be as cool and casual as possible. Kara and Blair hug me goodbye.

"I'll call you tomorrow," Blair says. "Bye Max! It was so nice to meet you!"

My friends bid Max farewell embracing him as if they've known him for years. Jayson and Max say their goodbyes and we get ready to head back to the car. But as we were about to make our great escape, I see Brandon turn around and catch us leaving.

Brandon says, "Damn Jade, leaving so soon? What's wrong, you afraid that I'm going to scare your new boy-friend away?"

His friends giggle in the background.

I turn around facing him, "Shut up Brandon."

Max looks at me and says, "Don't even worry about him."

Brandon chuckles, "Don't get mad at me." He puts his hands up as if he is surrendering, "I'm just saying."

Now Max is irritated, "What are you saying man?"

Brandon looks at Max and says, "I'd be careful with this one. She be on some hoe shit!"

And just like that, I lose my cool. My cup of delicious margarita leaves my hand and splashes all over Brandon's face. He's infuriated, his pale skin turning red. Next thing I know, he's lunging at me and Max lunges at him. Brandon's friends, Jayson, and some random bystanders jump in to separate them. All the commotion drew a lot of attention and event security made their way over, forcing us to break things up. Max quickly grabs my hand and leads me to the car. He was fuming, his steps matching his fury. I swear I could see the veins on the side of his neck popping out. I let him drag me along in silence, afraid of what to say. By the time we reach the car, I notice he's managed to calm down.

He leans up against his car and pulls me close to him, "So what was that about?"

I exhale, not at all surprised by his curiosity, "I dated him for a few months and he was not my cup of tea. So I broke things off and he didn't take it too well. He called me a bitch and I ended up slapping him."

Max intently listens then says, "Jade, you can't give assholes like that power over you to the point where you can't control your own actions. People like him feed off that shit; can't you see that? What if he actually put his hands on you? One of us would be going to jail right now."

I nod my head, embarrassed and ashamed of my actions, "You're absolutely right. I'm so sorry for even making you get involved in that."

I truly felt like an asshole. He was right; Brandon shouldn't be able to get that type of reaction out of me, especially since I don't give a shit about him. That situation could've gotten very ugly. What if Max or my friends got hurt? I nervously look down at my quivering hands and shake my head. Max can see that I was beating myself up about this.

He places his hand on my cheek, "It's ok Jade. I'm never going to let someone disrespect you on my watch, but just let me handle things next time."

I gaze into his eyes, more vulnerable than I've ever been comfortable with, "Ok."

Max leans down and kisses me on the forehead before helping me into the car.

4

I sleep peacefully, too peacefully. The smell of bacon tickles my nose, willing me to wake up. Naturally stubborn, I keep my eyes closed for a few more moments. I can feel the sunlight creep into the bedroom through the curtains. After a couple minutes pass, I finally accept that I'm officially awake for the day and reluctantly open my eyes.

I wake in Max's room for the fourth morning in a row. I'm sure Blu has a serious bone to pick with me for forcing him to sleep alone for so many nights. Max isn't in bed with me, knowing him he probably woke up early to work out or something. My phone goes off and I reach over to grab it from the nightstand.

ALEENA: WE'RE ON OUR WAY! CAN'T WAIT TO SEE YOU! XOXO

I quickly reply to her text and put my phone back down. Today was a big deal. It was our parent's 30th wedding anniversary. I stretch and ready myself for the day ahead. Peeling myself out of bed, I reach for one of Max's T-shirts and put it on. It was a habit I've grown accustomed to over the last few days.

I can't quite put my hand on it, but I can't get enough of him. Quite honestly, it is exciting but scary as hell. I find myself craving his company… all the time. That is just not like me. I mean by now, I would've found a reason to break things off. But things with him are everything I've ever wanted: companionship, romance, and most of all fun. I loved that he supported me and wasn't threatened by my drive or determination as far as my career was concerned. With the exception of our run-in with Brandon a few weeks ago, I'm on cloud nine literally all the time. Although I love the feeling, I'd be lying if I said I wasn't also petrified.

Downstairs I can hear the television and eggs frying. I walk into the kitchen and find Max, shirtless and sexy as ever, standing over the stove putting his final touches on our breakfast.

I walk up behind him and wrap my arms around his chest, "Good morning."

He turns to face me with a smile, "Morning sleepy head."

We share a quick kiss before he orders me to sit down. Moments later he joins me with two plates containing fried eggs, bacon and toast. We enjoy our breakfast with coffee and the morning news. Once finished, I gather our plates and take them over to the sink to wash them.

"So, what's the plan today?" Max asks.

"Well, I definitely have to go home and feed Blu," I explain. "Would you mind it if we slept at my place tonight? I'm afraid he feels neglected."

"Of course not." Max chuckles, "Poor Blu, I guess we have to share you."

I nod, "Yes, he's my baby. I know he misses me, I miss him too."

"Ok, so we're sleeping at your house tonight, what else?"

"Well, there's this thing," I pause, nervous and unsure of how to ask.

I've never really brought anyone to meet my family, not since high school at least. It's not that I was completely opposed to the idea, I just haven't liked someone long enough to bring them around. This was pretty new to me and honestly, I wasn't sure how to ask him.

He raises his eyebrow with curiosity, "You going to elaborate?"

I reply, "My parent's 30th wedding anniversary."

"Wow, that's amazing," he is genuinely impressed and equally excited.

I shrug, "Yea I guess, it wasn't always pretty."

Part of me feels guilty for my lack of enthusiasm; the other part had no desire to discuss my parent's rocky relationship.

"Nothing ever is. I can't help but notice that you don't seem too excited."

I shrug, "I guess I should be right?"

"Well I know I would be. Marriage, a strong marriage is something most people won't ever get to experience. Growing up it was just me and my mom, I never had the luxury of coming up in a two parent household and seeing what it takes to be married."

I listen stunned. Goodness I'm sure he thinks I'm a jerk. I mean, who am I to be so ungrateful? Yes my father left home, but he was still very much a big part of my life. Max wasn't that lucky, his father died before he was born. He never even got the chance to make memories or get to know his father. Before my parent's separation, I remember having some of the best memories of my dad. I was daddy's little girl; I just loved everything about him; his confidence, his strength and the way he took care of his family. When he and my mother reconciled, he was determined to right his wrongs and atone for his mistakes, but I never trusted him not to leave us again. Seeing that others are not as fortunate to have a father that actually came back, I realized that maybe I've been too hard on my dad over the years.

I can feel Max watching me.

"Well, would you like to come with me?" I ask, meeting his gaze.

"I'd be honored to," he replies with a smile.

We pull into the driveway of the country club and Max hands his keys to the valet. He helps me out of the car and we make our way through the marbled corridor. The building is lined with glass double doors that overlook the golf course and swimming pool. Moments later, we are greeted by a chipper club host.

She waves welcoming us, "Hi! Are you here for the James anniversary?"

I nod, "Yes we are."

She smiles, "Right this way."

She leads us down another corridor through a banquet room and then finally outside to the gathering. I look around and can't help but chuckle; this had my mother written all over it. The party is set up in a tent alongside a pond housing lily pads and exotic fishes. There's well-dressed wait staff serving food and beverages throughout the party, a DJ, and a decked out dessert bar. Walking hand in hand, Max and I join my parents and close family friends.

We near the dance floor and I quickly spot my parents dancing and embracing the spotlight. They're impeccably dressed; my mother is sporting a new haircut and a floor length form fitting dress, while my father rocks a white linen suit and fedora. Once my mother sees me she jumps with joy. She makes her way towards me and drags my father along. I greet them both with warm hugs and hand them their gift.

"Happy anniversary mom and dad," I say.

"Thank you darling," my mother beams.

My dad says, "It's about time you got here, everyone has been asking for you."

My mother looks at Max and smiles, "And who is this?"

Here goes nothing.

"Mom, dad this is Max. Max, this is my mother Michelle and my father Cliff."

Max smiles, "It's a pleasure to meet you Mr. and Mrs. James, congratulations on thirty years."

He shakes my mother and father's hands.

"Damn son, you've got one hell of a grip on you." My dad jokes, "Bout time you found yourself a real man Jade."

My cheeks flush.

"Oh stop it Cliff before you embarrass her," I hear my mom order.

It was too late, I was already embarrassed. Before I find an excuse to drag Max away and find the nearest escape, two hands cover my eyes taking me by surprise. I quickly grab them and turn around to see it's my sister Aleena and her husband Nate. We excitedly hug before I introduce them both to Max. They welcome him with open arms just like I knew they would. After some light chitchat, we make our way through the party and I introduce Max to about everyone I can before we take a seat and get something to eat.

I was wrapped up in a mindless conversation with one of my mother's coworkers when I overhear my father say, "So what are your intentions with my daughter?"

I cringe; my father was known for his straight shooter approach. Unfortunately, I had no choice but to sit back and hope Max makes it out alive.

Aleena joins my side, "Oh God, is dad starting his shit?"

"You know it."

"That man is hilarious. You might as well leave it alone for now, I'm sure Max will be fine."

I wryly grin, "I hope you're right."

Aleena gives me a reassuring smile. I can't help but notice her glow; marriage looks good on her. She looks phenomenal; her short pixie cut is sharp, complimenting her cheekbones and slender neck. She could give Halle Berry a run for her money.

"Ok short hair is definitely your thing," I observe.

She chuckles, "You think? I was thinking about growing my hair back out."

I quickly shake my head, "No! This is so you."

She ponders for a moment, "You're right I don't miss having to deal with hair. I don't know how you do it!" She stands on her feet, "Come with me to the bathroom."

I join my mother and sister in the bathroom to freshen up. My mother is powdering her nose and Aleena is reapplying her lipstick as I step out of the bathroom stall. I can feel them watching me as I go to wash my hands.

Aleena says, "Well, Max seems nice."

"He is," I smile.

My mother and sister continue to gape at my every move.

I reach for a folded towel and dry my hands, "What?"

"I haven't seen you take a guy this serious since Damon," my mother says.

"Yea, tell me about it," I snort.

"You're different," my sister adds.

I turn to her intrigued, "What do you mean?"

"You two are in sync. You move he moves, he moves, you move," my mom states.

I blush with a twinge of guilt. *Jeez is it that obvious?*

I ask, "And?"

Aleena is amused, "And what?"

My mother asks, "So you're alright with that?"

I turn to face my mother, "Well, yea I guess," I say.

Their prying was beginning to annoy me.

Almost instantly Aleena jumps to hug me, "He's the one! I know it!"

"What?" I say hugging her back.

"I'm so excited!"

"I love you both but can you please relax? I don't need the unnecessary pressure," I plead.

They smile and nod, sharing a sneaky look with each other.

I roll my eyes and go back outside to find Max, who's engaged in a conversation with Nate. I hand him the bottle of beer I grabbed him from the bar and he quickly kisses me on the forehead before wrapping his free hand around my shoulder.

"Jade, you didn't tell me you were dating Mr. Grand Artiste," Nate says.

I smile, "Well I didn't get a chance to. But he's quite amazing."

Nate nods in agreement. I can tell that he is eager to get to know Max better. I knew he was desperate for a male buddy in our family. It was a come up from only relying on interacting with our father, who could be quite the handful.

"But yea man, let me know when your next show is, I'm definitely trying to check it out. Shit I've wanted to get more into art anyway."

We chuckle, Nate was super nice and a constant jokester. That was one of the reasons my sister fell for him; he always knew how to make her smile. As the party dies down, Aleena's best friend Naomi arrives. After saying her hellos, she runs over to Aleena and I embracing us with excitement.

"Oh my goodness Naomi, you look stunning!" I say.

"No Jade that's you! You always look good!"

"She's aight," Aleena says.

We all giggle. By then, Naomi notices Max, who is engaged in guys talk with my uncles, father and Nate.

"Damn, who is that?"

"Hmm, ask Jade," Aleena says winking at me.

"Jade! That's you?" Naomi whispers.

I nod and blush, "That's Max and yes he is off limits."

"Oh shit! Well bringing him around the family is new isn't?"

"Yea it is, I think he could be the one girl," Aleena adds.

"Ha! Yea right," Naomi laughs.

"What's so funny?" I ask a bit offended by her response.

She looks at me, shocked that I was offended, "Well you know, you're Jade the heart-breaker. You love them and leave them and I love you for it!"

Naomi not only looked up to me as the older sister she never had, she also embraced my old lifestyle. When I was ready to throw in the towel, she was more than happy to take over the reins. Only this time, she was happily doing so in New York, a paradise for single girls.

"Naomi!" Aleena interjects.

"What? We aren't like you Aleena, some women simply aren't the marrying type."

I sit back, kind of stunned. Naomi was right; I was infamous for my intolerance. In doing so, I was always able to protect myself from getting in too deep and ending up hurt. Once I felt things getting too serious, I'd always find a way to get out. I look over at Max and he waves at me.

On our way back home, I'm consumed by my own thoughts. Something about what Naomi said had really gotten to me and I hoped to God that she was wrong. Because I knew that at this point in my life, with the right guy, I could become the "marrying type". A large part of me felt like I could be that with Max. He was so different; everything about him, the way he walks, the way he talks, the way he looks at the world, the way he now has me looking at the world, it's all so infectious. It all almost felt too good to be true.

"Everything ok?" he asks. "You're unusually quiet."

I smile, "Yes, I'm just tired."

He nods, placing his right hand on my thigh, while using his other hand to drive. The sun is setting and Benjamin Franklin Parkway looks magical as we make our way back to my place. We comfortably ride in silence listening to Emeli Sande' with the windows down. I close my eyes and enjoy the slight breeze that touches my face.

Upon reaching our destination, Max parks the car, gets out and opens the passenger door for me. We walk hand in hand towards my apartment building. The concierge smiles at us as we come through the doors and get onto the elevator. I lean up against the wall as he hits eight for my floor and settles up against the opposite wall facing me. It was a long day, long but amazing. Exhaustion was beginning to settle in; I close my eyes and roll my shoulders to stretch my neck a bit. Once I open them, I see that he's watching me.

Without saying another word, he pushes up against me putting his mouth on mine. Pinning me against the wall, he lets his tongue do a slow dance in my mouth. I lean into him, welcoming his advances. Max takes his free hand, places it under my sundress and slides it up my inner thigh. His fingers brush up against my womanhood and I let out a soft moan. Yearning for him to be inside of me, I gloat at my neglect to put on panties earlier that day. Then, the sound of the elevator indicates we've reached our floor. Reluctantly, we pull apart long enough to get off and walk to my apartment. Upon reaching the door, I pull out my keys and quickly unlock it. We walk inside and continue where we left off; I throw my arms around his neck as he grips my behind. He feels and tastes so good. Taking me by surprise, he sweeps me up off my feet and leads me into my bedroom without pulling away his kiss.

Placing me down onto the bed, he slowly slides my dress completely off, revealing my naked body. My breast stand at attention and the inside of my thighs grow moist with anticipation. I can see the bulge in his jeans through the dim streetlights. I lie there watching him with lust in my eyes. Max grabs my legs and pulls me to the edge of the bed. Leaning over me, he slowly traces his tongue across my neck to my collarbone, and then to my breasts before kissing me again. Taking a free hand he softly cups my breast and slides his other hand between my legs. Determined to finish what he started, he inserts his middle finger inside me; still kissing me, he slowly moves his finger in and out. I close my eyes and moan with pleasure.

"You're so wet baby," he whispers.

"It's your fault, I've wanted you all day," I whine.

I craved him so badly and he knew that. He was teasing me and it was sweet torture. Spreading my legs apart and getting onto his knees, he indulges in my sweet spot. He lets his tongue continue its seductive dance, pushing me to the edge. I cling to his head and raise my hips eager to meet his masterful tongue. Relishing the feeling, I bite my lip and touch my breasts. I can feel his eyes on me; he's watching my every move, refusing to pull away. My moans grow louder when he inserts two fingers inside of me while his tongue swirls around my clit. I can feel the deep pressure growing. Then before I can stop it, I explode and cry out with my blissful release.

Panting, I struggle to catch my breath. He stands up and removes his jeans, it was clear that he wasn't done with me yet. Eager to show my appreciation, I get up onto my feet and yank down his briefs. Dropping onto my knees, I eagerly take him into my mouth. He closes his eyes and tilts his head back reveling in the sensation of my tight wet mouth. I work my magic slowly bobbing my head with a strategic rhythm, teasing him by letting my tongue flick around the tip and blowing on it. He places his hand in my hair, and watches me with hunger in his eyes. I suck with passion and let my hands trail across his torso and hips.

Then, Max suddenly pulls away and swiftly lifts me up and I wrap my legs around him once more. He gently lays me back onto the bed kissing me passionately as I lift my hips and grind into his erection with fervor. Before I know it, he slides a condom on and slowly fills me inch by inch causing me to gasp; my heart races and I savor the feeling. His muscles flex as he straddles me, working his pelvis in a nice and easy rhythm. I pull him closer and he goes deeper. He cups my breasts and places them in his mouth as he continues to stroke in and out. I arch my back and close my eyes; with each thrust, he goes deeper and deeper; the feeling was electrifying.

I push him over straddling him, and I begin to wind my hips and moan with each movement. Max watches me work while his hands hungrily caress my body. I rock back and forth, my body glistening with sweat and lust; I can feel him hitting my spot. Max smacks my ass before reaching up to weave his fingers through my hair and pull me in for a deep kiss. He then drives his hips up meeting my thrusts, taking me completely by surprise. The sensation sent me over the edge and I can no longer control myself. In an instant, my breathing turns heavy and I pull from our feverish kiss to wrap my arms around his neck for support.

"I'm about to cum," I moan.

He responds by gripping my ass and pounding into me harder. My moans become louder and louder as I call his name. He increases his speed and I feel him grow larger inside of me. Then, we both cry out in orgasmic ecstasy together before collapsing and falling asleep in each other's arms.

***

"Daddy don't go," she cries clinging to her father's leg.

"I have to go Jade, go back into the house with your mother," Cliff responds.

"Daddy don't you love us anymore? I promise I will be a good girl."

Michelle calls out to her daughter, "Jade! Come inside!"

"Daddy please don't go!" Jade pleads.

"You see what you're doing to your children!" Michelle hisses at her estranged husband.

He picks Jade up, kisses her on the cheek and walks her back over to the porch before placing her down. He then walks over to his car where his companion is waiting. Jade's mother runs after him.

"Don't you dare bring that bitch over here again!" She says slapping at his back.

Cliff turns around blocking her attack. He grabs her by the wrists trying to subdue her aggression which only causes her to fall. Michelle cries out as he shakes his head with distaste and turns to leave. Jade and her sister Aleena run to their mother with tears in their eyes. Jade watches her father as he gets into the car and drives away with his girlfriend.

I wake up in a cold sweat. My chest heaves as I struggle to catch my breath. I turn and see Max sound asleep; completely unaware of the demons that haunt me, and that I sometimes forget haunt me myself. I study his face and wonder where this is going. I can't deny it; I was falling in love with him. But I was determined not to follow in my mother's footsteps and be played for a fool. I gently stroke his face and he opens his eyes.

"Hey," he whispers.

"Hey," I reply.

He opens up his arms inviting me to come lie back down. I smile before crawling up beside him and falling back to sleep.

5

A couple days pass and Max and I decide to go for a walk after dinner. Taking a tranquil stroll has quickly become one of our favorite things to do on a lazy evening. There was something about getting lost in the city while having enjoyable conversations and people watching that we both enjoyed. Right now we were involved in a heated debate regarding our favorite Hollywood actors.

I argue, "Listen, Leonardo DiCaprio is one of the best actors of our time!"

Max's mouth drops, "How can you sleep on Denzel? Have you seen his body of work? You're tripping."

I roll my eyes and take a scoop of my gelato. We continue our discussion before Max suddenly breaks his stride and turns toward me with a serious expression.

"I have a surprise for you."

He pulls out his phone and shows me a picture of a beautiful island. The water is crystal blue, the sand is white and there are palm trees lining the coast. He swipes left revealing another picture of a little house situated by the translucent ocean with a cabana and a hammock hanging on a tree.

I ask, "What's this?"

He answers, "A private house in Costa Rica."

I was intrigued and equally confused, "And why are you showing me this?"

"I got called there for some work and I'd love for you to join me," Max explains.

I smile, "Are you serious?"

He wraps his arm around me as we continue walking, "Yea silly."

"Ok, and you don't think I would distract you from your work?" I question.

"No not at all. In fact, I want to shoot you," he replies.

I nearly trip, "Shoot me? But I'm not a model."

"You don't need to be a model, you're you," he says looking into my eyes. "I love seeing you like this; comfortable in your own skin, everything about you is so alluring. I know that you'd make an amazing subject."

I smile; I was truly flattered by his offer and his keen observation of…me.

Max takes my hand, "Just say yes, it's already booked and taken care of."

I look at him stunned. Then finally I say, "When do we leave?"

"A couple of weeks," he answers.

I was at a loss for words; all I could manage was to look at him with shock written all over my face. No one had ever done anything like that for me and actually surprised me in such a way.

"So, will you come to Costa Rica with me Jade?"

"Yes!" I exclaim before jumping into his arms.

We giggle and hug like two people in love; the evening was turning out to be perfect. The sun begins to set and we opt to make our way back to the car and head home. Hand in hand, we discuss our upcoming trip and all the things we can do.

"So how about those swimming lessons? I can teach you," I say.

"I'll think about it," Max answers.

As we near my car, my phone starts ringing and I stop walking to quickly pull it out of my purse. I see it's my mother and answer at once.

"Hey mom, what's up?" I say, taking Max's hand again and continuing our walk.

"Jade, it's your father," my mother says.

"What's wrong mom?"

"He had a stroke, he's in the hospital."

"Oh my goodness!"

She sniffles, "He's in a coma."

I stiffen. Max stops, studying me.

"What hospital are you at?" I manage to ask.

"Pennsylvania, room two fifteen."

"Alright I'll be right there," I say before hanging up.

Max gently rubs my shoulders, "What's wrong?"

"It's my father," I utter. "He…he had a stroke and is in a coma."

His expression quickly changes from confused to worried, "I'm so sorry Jade."

I try to say something back but nothing comes out. I'm speechless, frozen in place. *Please Lord let my father be ok!*

Max can see the dread written all over my face, "Do you want me to come with you?"

I softly shake my head yes before bursting out into tears. Max promptly pulls me in for a hug.

We arrive at the hospital and anxiously walk to my father's room. My mother is sitting beside him, her head bent down and eyes closed, she's holding his hands and praying. When she hears us come in she quickly looks up.

"Oh!" She cries out and hops to her feet, pulling us in for a tight hug. She looks at Max, "Thank you for coming."

He gives her a reassuring smile.

I ask, "Has anything changed?"

She shakes her head no.

"What caused this?"

"They said that it's most likely stress. He's been working so much lately," my mom says.

"Yea that sounds like dad. Were you with him when it happened?"

"No, he was leaving work. It happened in the parking lot as he was walking to his car. Luckily his coworkers were there and called 911."

My mother couldn't hold back the tears any longer. I quickly give her another hug.

I say, "Hopefully we'll find out what's going on."

She nods her head, "They just finished running some tests, so we should know more soon."

She holds my hand and we take a seat next to the bed, Max follows.

"Did you call Aleena?" I ask.

"Yes, she's on her way with Nate now," she replies.

Distress took over my mother's face. I hated that I couldn't do anything to change it. All I could do was pray that my father pulls through, and comfort my mother as best as I knew how. A couple hours later, I just finished sending my boss Paul an email explaining my family's emergency and my need to take a few days off. When I put my phone down, Aleena and Nate finally arrive. They are visibly exhausted from the last minute trip; that D.C. traffic could be quite unforgiving. The mere sight of our father lying motionless in a hospital bed sends Aleena over the edge. My mother and Nate quickly pull her into the hallway and try to console her. Moments later, Max excuses himself to use the bathroom and to get us all some snacks, leaving me all alone with my comatose father.

I was actually thankful for the silence; I needed a moment to collect my thoughts and process everything. I close my eyes and rub my temples, desperate to find some clarity. Unfortunately, that was cut short by an obnoxiously loud ringtone. I squeeze my eyes shut and attempt to drown out the sound, but I'm unsuccessful. Agitated, I quickly search the room to find the source and realize it's coming from my dad's workbag. I guess in all the confusion the nurses just threw it wherever it landed. The sound was beyond annoying and seemingly never ending. I needed it to go away immediately.

I reach over to retrieve it out of the front pouch and quickly search for the silence button. My father resented technology (cell phones included) and only carried one because we made him. In doing so, he settled for an ancient flip-phone that had actual buttons on it. It was a far cry from the IPhone I've grown accustomed to, which explains why I had such a hard time finding the silence button. Before I was able to find solace in silence, I notice an unfamiliar name flash across the screen. *Who the hell is Tracy?* Against my better judgment, I quickly answer the phone.

"Hello?" I say.

"Can I speak to Cliff?" an unfamiliar voice says.

Stunned, I ask, "Who is this?"

"Who's this? "I could hear the sass in her voice.

"This is his daughter, now why the hell are you calling my father?"

Click.

The sound of the dial tone was more deafening than that exasperating ringtone. I instantly pull up Tracy's contact information to call her back and give her a piece of my mind. But before I could call her back and curse her the fuck out, Max and my family walk back into the room, forcing me to play it cool. Instinctively, I place my dad's phone in my back pocket. The last thing I needed was for that woman to call again and have my mother answer the phone.

Twenty long hours pass with no changes. We sit with my father, refusing to leave his side. This left me time to ponder over what the hell was going on. My mother said it herself: he was working all the time, he just had a stroke due to stress (I'm sure it's from living a double life), and then a mysterious woman is calling his phone. Given his cheating past, it was easy to come to one conclusion. I look at him, worried for his wellbeing but sickened by his character. It was all too much to try and digest, I needed to get out of there. But just as I was about to go outside for some fresh air, my father opens his eyes.

Max insisted on staying with me while we got my father situated. He was amazingly supportive and I was so grateful for his concern. But when it came time for my father to be released, I urged him to go home and get some rest. Hell, I felt horrible for having him tied up with my family at the hospital for over twenty-four hours. I promised him that I would call him once I got my father taken care of.

My father is sent home the next day with some medication and a warning to slow down. He was ordered to take it easy over the next few weeks and to try to find ways to minimize his stress. Once we arrive at my parent's house, my mother jumps right into making my father feel comfortable. She makes him take a seat in his favorite re-cliner, puts his feet up and brings him some warm tea. I can see that my dad loved all the attention.

"I'm starving," my dad announces.

At once, my mother is on her feet, "What do you want honey?"

"Ribs and cornbread," he answers almost instantly.

We all burst out in laughter. His request lightened the mood although it was a bit unexpected for someone that was just in a coma. But my mom was determined to give him whatever he wanted and places an order for baby-back ribs from our favorite local soul food restaurant without a second thought. Aleena and Nate volunteer to pick up the order, leaving my parents and I alone. Since Aleena refused to go back to D.C. until they were absolutely certain that dad was alright, my mother heads upstairs to get Aleena's old room together so that she and Nate would be comfort-able during their stay. I figured it was something to do to keep herself occupied and not hovering over my father.

Now that we were alone, I struggled with how to best handle the situation. One thing that I knew was that my dad was up to no good. And I was willing to bet that my mother had no clue. I also knew that I couldn't force him to be a standup guy and do right by her, but I wanted an-swers. The logical side of me resolved that today was not the time to get the answers I was seeking, especially since my father was in such a fragile state. Instead, I decide to go home; I wanted nothing more than to shower, call Max, and to snuggle up with Blu.

"Alright dad, I'm going to head home," I say before getting up and giving him a quick peck on the cheek.

"Ah don't leave, you're going to miss the food," he protests.

I shake my head to decline, "I'm not that hungry."

Before turning to leave, his cell phone rings again. I take it out of my back pocket and see Tracy on his caller ID. Disgusted, I place the cell on his recliner's armrest. My father casually picks it up and flips it open before rejecting the call.

"Aren't you going to answer that?"

He shakes his head, "Not in the mood for calls from work."

I snort and mumble, "Yea I bet."

He looks at me confused, or at least he was acting confused. I couldn't be around him anymore, pretending to be something we were not. I needed to know the truth.

"Are you having an affair?"

The bluntness of my question completely throws him off. He stares at me, trying to figure out what I know.

After what feels like an eternity, he finally says, "What's wrong with you Jade?"

"Dad, please don't try and change the subject. I'm not a kid anymore, please tell me the truth," I pause. "Who is Tracy? And why is she calling you?"

His eyes grow big and I'm sure his blood pressure has spiked by now.

"Where do you get off talking to me like that? I'm your father, and what I do with my life is none of your damn business."

At that exact moment, my mother walks back into the living room. By the look on her face I could tell she heard part if not all of our conversation, "Jade, your father just left the hospital! Why are you trying to upset him?"

Shocked, I turn and look at her disgusted, "Why are you always defending him?"

"He's my husband Jade, you wouldn't understand."

Even though I don't think she meant it, my mother's words definitely hit a sore spot. So now because I'm not married I don't understand when a man doesn't treat a woman right? I could feel myself becoming angry.

I turn to her and say, "No I guess I don't. But what's the point of having a husband if he makes you look so weak? Get a grip mom, you're so pathetic!"

I couldn't bear to be around them any longer, the sight of my fucked up parents made me sick. Before either of them can stop me, I grab my bag and leave. Enraged, I hop into my Audi and speed off. An all too familiar feeling creeps over me and just like that, I feel like I'm a helpless eight-year-old again. I needed Max; I needed to be around someone that would make me feel better. I activate my car's Bluetooth and prompt it to dial Max's number. After a few rings, it goes to voicemail. I hang up and direct my phone to call again. No answer. Before I know it, I need to pull over and regain control of my tears.

6

The next day, I wake feeling mentally drained. I know that I desperately need to take some time to recharge my batteries before I can face the realities of my life. The pounding in my head makes me regret choosing to drown my sorrows with a bottle of wine the night before. Thank goodness it's Saturday. I find some comfort in knowing that I don't have to make up some ridiculous excuse for missing work.

My cell goes off and it's a call from Max. I let it ring, contemplating whether I should answer or not. Once the ringing stops, I place it on the "Do Not Disturb" mode and stuff it away in my nightstand drawer. A familiar feeling of restlessness has taken over me and I can't seem to shake it. I roll over and stroke Blu, tormented by what I was going to do. Ever since storming out of my parent's house last night, I can't help feeling that I have to let Max go.

Yes, he was an amazing man; and for a moment there I actually thought I would get my happy ending. When

I'm with him, it's so easy to forget about everything else. I haven't allowed anyone to get this close to me in such a long time. The last time I did, I ended up shattered with a broken heart. Not having him in the moment I needed him most was an extreme wake up call and a brutal reminder of what being abandoned felt like. Last night I was faced with the harsh reality that I can't count on anyone. That, coupled with having a front row seat to my parent's rocky marriage, added to my fear of ever really opening up my heart to anyone else. Max came along and had me wide open. Knowing that scared me to my core, it made me feel helpless and paralyzed.

I tossed and turned all night, haunted by the realization that what I had with Max couldn't possibly last forever. Now thoughts that I've tried to ignore are ringing loudly throughout my head. Like, where is this going? Will we end up like my parents? Is he truly good for me? What if someone better comes along? If I'm being honest with myself, I've tried for weeks to ignore these notions, but I feel like I'm suffocating and I longed for the chance to merely breathe. I pull myself out of bed and feel sluggish; coffee is an absolute must today.

By noon, I was three episodes into my newfound favorite Netflix series, *The Crown*. I was just about to get up and fix myself a bowl of ice cream when I hear a knock at my front door. I quickly pause the show and make my way towards my entrance. When I open the door, I come face to face with Max. He smiles and I try my best to return the favor, we share a brief kiss before he walks in.

"I'm sorry I missed you last night, I left my phone at my studio and didn't get it back till this morning," he explains.

I look down, nervously biting my lip.

"Jade, what's wrong? Did something happen with your father?"

I briskly shake my head, "I don't want to talk about it."

Naturally, Max tries to console me by rubbing my shoulders.

He says, "Well do you want to do something to take your mind off things? Pick a spot for lunch, my treat."

I release myself from his hold, "I can't go with you Max."

I spoke so low that I could barely hear my own words. Max looks at me, clearly hearing what I said; I can see he's confused.

"What do you mean? Is something wrong?"

I hesitate, contemplating my next move.

He presses, "Are you sick?"

I struggle to find the right words, "No not exactly."

Max takes my hand, leads me to the couch and we both take a seat.

He looks at me, his eyes filled with worry, "Jade, talk to me. What's wrong?"

"I needed you last night Max. I needed you and you weren't there for me, you weren't there when I needed you the most," I can feel the tears forming. "I've given this whole thing a lot of thought and I can't do this anymore."

Max now looks surprised, "What do you mean you can't do this anymore?"

I exhale and my eyes fixate onto my feet.

"Jade," he says with a little more assertiveness.

"Look Max, I just want to be friends."

I look up and can tell he's taken aback by my words. Shit, I can't even believe what I'm saying, but it's like word vomit and I can't stop it. Unable to look him in the eye, I get up and pace the living room. He remains on the couch, unsure of what to say or do next. Then finally, he sinks his head into his hands, defeated.

After a moment, he looks up and says, "I don't need any more friends Jade. I'm sorry I wasn't there for you last night, but I think you're overreacting. Let's talk about this."

I plead, "Max please don't make this any more difficult than it already is."

"Why can't you let me in?" he says, standing up.

I instantly stop pacing and look at him, "Because I already know how this ends."

"You don't know a damn thing," he says.

I can tell he is starting to get irritated.

I shake my head, "I can't do this Max."

"That's not a fucking excuse! How about you admit it, you're scared that this actually might work and you're running!"

"I'm not scared, I'm smart" I lie. "I have things in my life I need to focus on, things you clearly are too busy for."

Max doesn't buy it. He can tell that I was doing everything in my power to push him away.

"Bullshit! Why are you so quick to end things? So you're telling me that this whole thing was for nothing? That you don't think every moment of what we have is great?"

I can't deny that. I simply nod my head.

"Yes Max, it was good, but then what? I give up my life and all that I have worked hard for just to be your chick? What then? You shit on me and break my heart when the next best thing comes along?" I quickly shake my head and continue, "I refuse to give you the power to hurt me!"

"Hurt you? Why would I want to hurt you Jade? I made an honest mistake, I'm human like you and I'm damn sure not perfect. But neither are you; you can be an over analytical brat sometimes but I think you are an amazing woman, and I know we could be amazing together. I know you feel it too," Max says.

I answer, "I did feel it."

"Then why are you doing this? What are you so afraid of?"

"Settling," I say. I can no longer deny the truth.

"So you think you're settling?"

"Yes."

He stares at me dumbfounded, my words cutting him like a knife. At that moment I know that I've pushed him away. A few moments pass before he finally turns and walks towards the door.

"You're so lost Jade," Max says before walking out of my apartment and slamming the door behind him.

It's been days since Max stormed out of my place. Although I've tried to ignore it, I can't help but wonder if I truly messed up and took things too far this time. Normally after dumping a guy, I'm able to bounce back and continue living my life without missing a beat. These last few days, however, have been the longest of my life. I find myself second-guessing my actions, tormented over my decision to end things so soon. I think about him more often than I should, even going as far as picking up the phone a few times to call him before my stubbornness stops me. By the weekend I was going stir crazy, trying to find any and everything to distract me from the internal tug of war I was feeling. A last minute invitation to a concert with Kara was exactly what I needed. When I get into her car, I can tell that she wanted to let off some steam.

"Hey girl," I say once seated inside.

We lean in kissing each other on the cheek.

She smiles, "Hey boo, thanks for coming with me."

"No, thank you for inviting me! I was desperate for something to do. I was beginning to lose my mind at home," I say with a chuckle.

We ride in silence for a moment.

"Still haven't talked to Max?" Kara asks, breaking the ice.

I swiftly shake my head no, "It's for the best."

"Yea? I don't know; I really liked him for you Jade."

I fasten my seat belt, refusing to feed into her stance on the matter. She and Blair gave me an earful when I finally broke the news to them. They instantly knew I found some reason to break things off with yet another suitor when I told them that we stopped talking.

I was in no mood to hear another lecture. So before Kara can say anything else, I opt to change the subject, "How are things with Rashad?"

She shakes her head annoyed, "We were supposed to go to this show tonight, planned it for weeks, but he cancelled this morning."

"Damn that sucks. Why?"

"Work, he has some major listings he needs to close out."

Kara has been dealing with Rashad for over a year. I've only met him a handful of times and I feel like I already have him figured out. While Kara is head over heels for this guy, I don't see nearly the same enthusiasm or commitment to the relationship from him. It's always the same story; he's always too busy and never willing to put Kara first.

She shakes her head again, clearly frustrated, "Honestly, I'm sick of this Jade. Things will be going so good and then he just switches up. He becomes distant and claims that relationships aren't his thing. It's like he punishes me for liking him, but when I try to move on he comes back around and treats me like a princess forcing me to fall for him all over again."

"I understand, you and Rashad have been doing the same dance for a while now. He obviously doesn't appreciate you, so why do you keep doing this to yourself?"

My heart truly ached for Kara. She was such a good person that had so much love to give. The fact that a person as caring as her had such a struggle in the dating world was really upsetting. Here she was desperately trying to find love, while I was just disposing of guys like clockwork.

"I know that. But he really makes me feel different. You know I've tried getting over him, but I just can't."

"You deserve to be with someone that's going to put you first."

"Yea I know, but I'm not done with him yet. I don't know, I think every girl has that one guy that makes her forget all logic you know. I guess Rashad is mine," she shrugs.

"And you're ok with that?"

She shrugs, "For now I guess. I'm not you Jade."

"What's that supposed to mean?"

"It means that I want the fairytale. I want someone to be all about me, I'm addicted to feeling…wanted. Rashad gives me just enough to keep me under his spell. You're different, the moment a guy shows genuine interest in you, you go running for the hills. You can't be tamed," she simply states.

I can't be tamed? I sit back, perplexed by her rationalization. A few years ago, I might've taken that as a compliment. But for some reason what she said stung. Was it true? Since having my heart broken (I was young and obviously naïve), I don't think I've ever allowed myself to be played for a fool by anyone else. I always prided myself on that. But now I can't help but wonder if my intolerance for pain has prevented me from ever finding what I truly want. Something real, something special, and something that is undeniable with someone else.

At the show, Kara and I are happy to forget about our problems and have a little fun. Jill Scott hits the stage and we have the best time singing and dancing along. But as the night goes on I can't shake what Kara said in the car. Everything that happened, my entire dating life, had me reevaluating a lot of things. Was I too hard to tame? I mean, had my resistance to vulnerability finally screwed me over? Was this the reason I pushed everyone away?

Once home, I immediately remove my clothes and makeup before hopping into the shower. The steam from the hot water instantly soothes my skin and helps me to center my thoughts. I was desperate to put all that happened behind me and move on. I refused to believe that my love life was doomed because I had standards. Relaxed and seeing clearer, I perform my nighttime routine and get into bed.

Gratefully exhausted from the day, I close my eyes and will myself to fall asleep. But half an hour later, sleep continued to evade me. I desperately try to find comfort so that I can fall into a deep, much desired slumber. After allowing a few more moments to pass, I sit up aggravated and restless. The last thing I wanted to do was think of him and let regret creep over me once more. A true creature of habit, I reasoned the best way to get over a man was to get a new one. In an instant, I re-download the Tinder app, upload a new picture and sift through potential matches until I fall asleep.

2

It's Monday evening and I'm running late. Blair was performing some of her poetry for an open-mic night at one of the local bars in town. I promised her I'd make it, but work got super hectic and before I knew it, the day had escaped me. It was now seven o'clock and the show started in thirty minutes. I shut down my laptop and pull out my compact to check myself, quickly applying some lipstick and mascara. *Blair is going to kill me.*

Three weeks have passed and things are finally getting back to my normal pre-Max days. I went on a few dates, but nothing serious. If I'm being honest with myself, none of them were right. That, and deep down I knew that I just wasn't interested. By my fourth date, I was extremely underwhelmed. Guys nowadays seem so one-dimensional. It's always the same thing; they're either up to no good, into you for only one thing, or complete jerks. Unfortunately, I've encountered all the above in recent weeks. Nonetheless, I wasn't that put off to turn down free drinks and have an excuse to get out of the house. As I approach the elevator, my phone goes off and I know it's either Blair or Kara questioning my whereabouts, I was supposed to meet them twenty minutes ago.

Kara: WHERE THE HELL ARE YOU? IT'S ABOUT TO START!

I rush out of the elevator and stagger towards the building's exit. Pushing through the double doors, I begin typing my response.

Jade: I'M LEAVING THE OFFICE NOW.

Before I can hit send; I run right into what feels like a brick wall. The impact was so hard it causes me to stumble a bit, dropping my purse and all its contents inside: my lipstick, keys, and a loose tampon. Embarrassed, I quickly drop down on the sidewalk to retrieve my possessions.

"Jade? Jade James?" A deep yet familiar voice says.

I look up, and it's Damon. Damon fucking Wilson. The Damon Wilson that left me broken-hearted a decade ago. I look into his eyes and memories of our young love rush over me. I forgot how easy it was to get lost in those fucking enticing gray eyes. Time definitely was on his side; he looks damn good, almost too good for comfort. Since splitting up, I vowed to never be anyone's fool ever again. As Kara said, every girl has that one guy that they lose all sense of logic for and Damon was definitely my vice. Seeing him, and being in his presence brought back memories I desperately tried to forget. But here he was, in the flesh. I break his trance over me and quickly stuff my contents back into my purse.

"Hello Damon! What a pleasant surprise. What are you doing back in Philly?" I boast, standing upright.

"My job transferred me a couple weeks ago," he smiles as he helps me regain my balance.

Oh my goodness please don't tell me his job is in the same building as mine!

"Well what brings you here?" I ask.

He chuckles lightly, "I'm meeting up with a work buddy for drinks. Bumping into you was definitely a coincidence."

Relieved, I casually say, "Oh ok."

"What about you?"

"I'm also heading out to meet some friends." I check my watch, "Which I'm extremely late for."

"Oh don't let me hold you. My boy is actually waiting for me now."

"Well it was nice running into you," I say, determined to play it cool.

Damon asks, "How about you take my number and hit me so we can catch up?"

"Really?"

"Yea, we can be friends right?"

I shrug, "Yea I guess there's no harm in that."

He pulls out a business card and hands it to me before we share a brief hug and he smiles, "Well, I guess I'll see you around Ms. James."

7

It took me exactly three days before I finally decided to take Damon up on his offer. Now I know that may not seem like the smartest thing to do, especially considering the way we ended. But after much thinking, I realized that was the exact reason why I needed to call him. In a nutshell; Damon was the root of my problems. Because of him, I've never been able to find anyone who was exactly what I wanted. He was smart, charismatic, good-looking, and highly successful. (Thanks to my Facebook stalking I was able to see what Damon has been up to throughout the years.) Since we ended, I secretly imagined when we would cross paths once again. I promised myself that if that day ever came, I would take pleasure in showing Damon all that he missed out on and make him regret leaving me in the first place. Doing so would give me the much-desired closure that I've been seeking for so long.

I have to admit, I was extremely nervous when I dialed his number at first. After the third ring I contemplated hanging up and forgetting the entire thing.

"Hello?" Damon says through the line.

I say, "Hey Damon, it's me Jade."

"Jade! It's about time you called," he answers.

In no time we're completely immersed in our conversation. Over the years, Damon really made something out of himself like I always knew he would. After graduating college, Damon ventured to the West Coast and landed a job with one of the top pharmaceutical companies in the country. There, he built up his net worth and impressed some important people. Now at the age of thirty, he's being groomed to be his company's Chief Financial Officer.

Damon is equally impressed by my accomplishments. But he finds it hard to believe that I hadn't been in a serious relationship since we parted ways. Never one to waste time, Damon suggests hanging out as soon as possible. We agree to meet at Lucky Strike to engage in some bowling, drinking and more conversation. Once there, we rent our bowling shoes and walk to our assigned lane. I take a seat and he grabs a menu.

"What would you like to drink?"

"Um," I say reaching for the menu and quickly scanning it. "I'll take a Pinot Grigio."

We begin to put our shoes on and a waitress approaches us. She's clearly mesmerized by Damon's good looks. I instantly remember the effect he had on me when I first laid eyes on him and snicker at the thought. His lean muscles and curly hair definitely made him easy on the eyes. He dutifully orders our drinks and appetizers before she glides away.

"So, do you still suck at bowling?" he asks.

"Shut up, I'm not that bad," I chuckle.

He playfully rolls his eyes, "Yea, we'll see about that."

We giggle and the waitress arrives with our drinks.

Damon stands up and gestures towards the lane, "Ladies first."

I stand and walk towards the ball dispenser in our lane. I lean down looking for a ball, finally grabbing the lightest one I can find. Taking my place, I grasp the ball and take a deep breath. I take a few quick steps forward, simultaneously swinging my arm back to aid in my delivery, and forcefully release the ball. I stand there, willing it to roll down the lane towards the pins. Instead, it glides to the far right, resulting in a gutter ball. I turn to see Damon smiling and I shrug. Luckily I get one more chance to score. My second time around, I'm more comfortable and bowl a strike. Proud of myself, I arrogantly turn around and walk back towards my seat.

"Oh shit, I see you came to play! I hope you remember that I don't like to lose," he says.

"Yea I remember, bring it on," I flirt, ready for the challenge.

He takes another sip of his drink and hands it to me before rubbing his hands together and strutting towards the lane. Damon was very confident; his movements smooth and assuring. Rolling the ball, he knocks down nine pins. Smiling, he looks back at me giving me a quick wink and I wink back. By now, our waitress returns with a vast array of unhealthy goodness: mozzarella sticks, Buffalo wings, and quesadillas. I make a mental note to go to the gym the next morning.

Our date goes without a hitch. It feels like we are teenagers again, without a care in the world. After rolling my tenth gutter, I opt to take a seat and enjoy my drink and food. Bowling clearly isn't my thing and I am perfectly fine with that. I kick off my bowling shoes and relax a bit.

"Remember when you ripped your jeans climbing out your bedroom window?" Damon says as he takes a seat next to me.

We both burst out laughing.

I shake my head, "Oh my goodness! Yes, that was so embarrassing!"

"Man those were some good times," he says.

I nod in agreement. Suddenly the mood turns serious, I can't help but wonder why things had to end if they were so good. I mean, yes we were young but sometimes young love is everlasting. It seems to be working out for Aleena and Nate.

"Why did we break up?" The words leave my mouth quicker than I would like.

Damon sips his drink, deliberating my question, "I think when we got together; we got so serious so fast. It kind of scared me towards the end; especially with us going away to college and whatnot. I felt like I owed it to myself and to you, to give us a chance to actually live our lives and see the world you know?"

His answer leaves me stunned, but it makes complete sense. I realized it gave me the closure that I needed.

"Yes I understand that now."

Damon gently takes my hand and looks into my eyes with sincerity, "I'm so sorry for hurting you Jade. I never stopped thinking about you."

Every word he spoke was like music to my ears. I believed him and I knew that was all I needed to hear to let my guard down.

"I never stopped thinking out you either," I confess.

This was definitely not a part of my plan.

There are so many things I need to do; yet so little time. A couple days ago, Damon invited me for a night out. He refused to tell me where we were going; instead insisting that it was a surprise and suggesting that I get a cocktail dress. Never one to turn down a night of fun, I follow his instructions and spend the day getting ready (the works: hair, nails, and Brazilian wax). By the time I got home, I was ready to take a quick nap before getting dressed.

It's been a few weeks since Damon and I reconnected and I couldn't be happier. I know that this is a far cry from my initial intentions, but I can't help it. I find myself eager to spend as much time with him as I can, which is not always easy because of his job. Nonetheless, I felt like things were beginning to look up.

My time to gloat comes to an abrupt end once I pick up my cell and see three missed calls from my mother. Since our blow up, I hadn't talked to either of my parents much. I figured today was as good as any to smooth things over. Once in my apartment, I place my shopping bags down and call her back. She answers after the first ring.

"Hello Jade," my mother answers.

"Hi mom, is everything alright? I saw your missed calls. Is dad ok?"

She sniffles and I can tell that she's been crying.

"Mom, what's going on?"

"I think you were right, your father is having an affair."

I sigh, "I'm so sorry mom. How did you find out?"

"A few days after you left the house, I grew suspicious. I noticed he's always taking calls and going into the other room or stepping outside. So I looked through his phone the other night and saw that he keeps talking to this woman named Tracy. I needed to know the truth. So I followed him and I caught him meeting up with her for dinner."

I nearly choke, "Wait, you what?"

"I needed to know the truth," she repeats.

I listen stunned. I hate that I was right, and most of all that my mother was hurting.

"Mom, I'm sorry for blowing up at you the way I did. I should've never disrespected you. If you need anything, or want to come and stay at my place for a while let me know," I say.

My mother replies, "Thank you Jade, I appreciate that. I'm sorry for not believing you."

After a few minutes of some more chitchat, we hang up.

Damon takes my hand, helping me out of the car. I'm wearing a strapless Calvin Klein cocktail dress and peep toe pumps, while he dons a tailored grey suit paired with a crisp white shirt. A valet driver takes the keys from him and hops into the car.

"You're still not going to tell me where we're at?" I ask.

He shakes his head, "Nope."

I chuckle and we walk hand in hand inside the secret location. We're in Rittenhouse; the streets are filled with other couples and people eager to enjoy the beautiful summer evening. We pass a large mirror in the lobby and I notice our reflection; I can't help but to admire how good we look together. Once we get off the elevators, a red carpet leads us inside to an extravagant business gala. Servers wearing white suits are stationed throughout the space holding trays of expensive champagne. Damon goes to retrieve some and leaves me to admire the decor. There are massive swan ice sculptures, tall ivory candles, and immaculate floral arrangements strategically placed throughout the space. There's a live band playing soft music in the background. I can't help but to appreciate how elegant everything was. When Damon returns with two glasses in hand, we toast and take a sip to the night ahead.

With his hand secured on the small of my back, Damon glides me throughout the party. Together, we work the crowd, Damon introducing me to his colleagues, and most trusted mentors. The conversations are friendly and light as we get acquainted. Seeing him in this element was very admirable; he was at ease, extremely charming, and undeniably professional. He looks at me and sees me watching him, then cracks a smooth smile. I blush and sip my drink.

"Ladies and gentlemen, please take your seats. Dinner is served!"

I take my arm and loop it through Damon's as he leads me to our seats. After a moment, we find a table with a small white place card that says "Damon Wilson and Guest" in elegant gold script. Walking around me, he pulls out my chair and I take a seat before he follows suit. The formally arranged tables and chairs are draped with crisp white linens, crystal glasses, and exquisite centerpieces. I notice another card placed on the table inscribed with more gold writing, our dinner menu. Moments later, about thirty servers fill the room, greeting party guests and serving our first course.

Once dinner was over, I managed to meet more of Damon's associates and we danced the night away. The night was truly amazing; I could only hope that it would get better. During the car ride home, I'm quiet but anxious, mesmerized by my magical evening. The thought of him coming back to my place sent butterflies through my stomach.

"Did you enjoy yourself?" He says, interrupting my thoughts.

I look at him and smile, "I did, thank you for inviting me."

He winks at me as he pulls in front of my building, but for some reason he doesn't park.

"Don't you want to come up?" I ask.

"I'd love to, but I have an early flight to catch in the morning."

"Oh."

Damon immediately senses my disappointment, "It's a work thing, but trust me if I could I would love nothing more than to join you."

"Ok," I say as I begin to get out of the car.

Damon stops me and says, "I'm so glad we are back in each other's lives."

And just like that, my disappointment quickly evaporates, "Me too."

Then Damon grabs my hand, pulls me close and kisses me, causing me to lose my train of thought.

When we pull away I am breathless, "Goodnight Damon."

"Goodnight gorgeous. I'll call you when I'm back in town."

"Please do," I say before I open the car door and get out.

A few days later, Damon arrives at my place. Before letting him in, I stop and take one final look in the mirror. I'm wearing my favorite lounge set: simple, cute and tight enough to show off my curves. I open the door and he's standing there holding a bottle of wine. After letting him inside, I greet him with a hug and a kiss before taking the bottle and walking it to the kitchen. He gets comfortable and takes a seat on the couch while I grab the corkscrew from the pantry drawer and two wine glasses. After opening the wine, I pour our drinks then settle back into the living room. Damon turns on *Kill Bill Vol. 1* as I place our glasses down and take a seat next to him.

The movie plays and we get cozy sipping our wine. I try to focus on the movie but fail. Before I know it, my glass is already empty. I get up to grab the wine from the kitchen and bring it into the living room. Sitting back down, I pour myself another glass before getting comfortable with Damon. As much as I loved this movie and watching Uma Thurman show up and kick ass, I had other things in mind. I snuggle closer to him and he puts his arm around me. Sadly, he was still too focused on the movie. Determined as ever to get what I want, I place my hand on his leg and stroke it, forcing him to turn his attention on me.

He looks at me smiling, "What's up beautiful?"

Without saying a word, I pull him in for a kiss. Our tongues wrestle and I can taste the wine on his lips. I move my hand up his thigh and feel an erection growing. Damon puts his hand on my neck and kisses me back passionately. The way he kissed me turned me on in the worst way. Without hesitation, I straddle him as he grips me by the hips. We carry on this way for a few moments but then, to my surprise, Damon hops onto his feet and carries me into the bedroom. He lays me back onto the bed and climbs on top of me; this is exactly what I've been waiting for. Eager to feel him inside of me, I reach for his shirt and pull it off, and then I undo his pants before tugging them down. He assists me out of my clothes and our kiss grows deeper causing my thighs to become moister by the minute.

"Do you have a condom?" I whisper.

He shakes his head, "No, I wasn't expecting this to happen."

We both hesitate, unsure of what to do next. I sigh and bite my lip in contemplation.

"I'm on the pill," I finally say.

And without another word he's back kissing me. I reach for his penis and stroke it against my womanhood. I continue this tease until I can't take it anymore and slide him inside of me. He kisses my neck and begins to stroke slowly. I moan with pleasure and then push him onto his back and take my place on top. But to my surprise, his erection is gone.

He looks up at me embarrassed, "Shit, my bad."

I smile and scoot down, taking him into my mouth. After about ten minutes of doing my absolute best work, he's still flaccid. Defeated, I lie on my back.

"Is something wrong?" I ask.

"I think it's the wine," he says.

"Are you sure it's not me?"

He gets up pulling his boxers and jeans on and then leans in to kiss me, "You're perfect Jade."

I fake a smile, but I can't help but feel like that wasn't true. I mean, I've never had this issue before. Lost for words, I put on my clothes in silence and go into the bathroom to wash my face. Once finished, I walk out into the living room to see Damon fully dressed and standing by the door.

"You're leaving? What about the movie?"

"I have an early meeting tomorrow," he explains.

I sigh, "Ok."

I walk over to where he's standing and he leans in kissing me tenderly, "I'll call you tomorrow."

I open the door and he gives me another kiss on the cheek before leaving. Confused and mildly pissed off, I close the door behind him.

8

Ever since Damon left my apartment, I've barely talked to him. It's like the slight mishap the other night drove a wedge between us. I mean I've called and texted; but all I get are bullshit responses saying he was tied up with work. By the fourth day I was fed up and extremely perplexed. Not to toot my own horn, but I'm the one that's used to being chased, not the other way around. I felt vulnerable and was not too fond of the feeling. Frustrated, I pick up my IPad and quickly type up an email.

> **To: Damon Wilson**
> **From: Jade James**
> **Subject: Are we good?**
>
> **Hey, I'm getting really worried. Is every-thing ok? If this is about the other night**

can we please forget about it and start over?

Let me know...
JJ

After hitting send, I frantically tap my leg and nervously bite my bottom lip. For the record, this is so not my style. Suddenly, I hear a knock at my door. *It's Damon!* I hop up and scramble towards the doorway, opening it in a hurry. As soon as I do, my heart sinks.

"Hey Kara," I say, letting her in.

"Damn what's wrong with you?" She says as she walks into my apartment.

I settle on to the couch with her, picking up Blu and placing him in my lap, "Damon! He's being weird."

"Oh my goodness," she says rolling her eyes. Kara clearly thinks I am being ridiculous.

I sigh, "I thought things were cool, and then all of a sudden he's acting super distant."

"Jade, I'm sure everything is fine. From what you told me, things with you two have been going great."

"Yea, but I've been down this road before with him Kara. Remember when you said every girl has that one guy that they lose all common sense for? Well Damon is it for me. I can't do that again, if he's done I just need to know." I shamefully shake my head, "I kind of want to drop by his job and see what's up."

Kara's eyes widen in shock, "Girl, are you crazy? Don't do that. I wouldn't even do that shit."

A faint ring goes off on my IPad indicating a new email. I reach and grab it off the coffee table, swiping right to unlock the screen. Thankfully it's a reply from Damon.

> **To: Jade James**
> **From: Damon Wilson**
> **Subject: All good...**
>
> **Hey Jade, everything is good. I'm sorry I've been so busy with work. I'm out of town on business but let's go out when I get back...**
>
> **P.S. I miss you...**
> **D**

Once I finish reading his reply, I pass it to Kara.

She quickly reads it and hands the IPad back to me, "Everything seems fine to me."

I shrug.

"What's gotten into you? I've never see you tripping off a guy."

I close my eyes and rub my temples. She was right, I was tripping. But something just didn't seem right.

"Something is wrong, I can feel it."

"Seriously Jade, relax!" Kara says with a soft nudge.

My irrational behavior forces Kara to call an intervention, otherwise known as retail therapy. Relieved and ready to spend some of my hard earned money, I insist that Blair joins us. At the mall, Kara wastes no time telling Blair about my behavior. Blair stays silent, studying me; she was more than familiar with my history with Damon. When I initially told her that we reconnected, she wasn't exactly thrilled. Naturally, I merely shrugged it off and reasoned that she was being protective, that along with the fact that she still had hope that Max and I would work things out.

Blair asks, "When did he start acting weird Jade?"

Embarrassed, I reluctantly explain what happened.

Blair listens and she looks equally as confused as I was, "And you think he switched up cause of that?"

Kara snorts, "Blair she's tripping, please don't feed into her madness. That man is fine."

"I didn't think what happened was a big deal," I sigh. "I thought that was normal sometimes. But he never wants to have sex; all we ever do is kiss. It's not like we've never had sex before, I have history with this guy. He was my first for goodness sake."

"Now that's weird," Blair observes.

"See! So I'm not psychotic. Maybe he's embarrassed about something," I reason. "Or maybe I turn him off."

"Ok Jade, please stop you're talking crazy now," Kara orders.

Goodness I sound pathetic.

We stop at the food court for a quick snack, settling on fresh fruit smoothies. As we make our way through the rest of the mall, I mindlessly sip my banana berry concoction and check my phone.

Kara says, "Isn't that Max?"

I instantly stop walking and look up. There he was, walking hand in hand with a pretty girl. She's brown skinned, petite, and had a bright smile. The two look extremely happy as they make their way into Lord & Taylor department store. I take another sip of my beverage and can feel Kara and Blair's eyes on me.

"What?" I ask.

They wait.

I sigh, "I'm fine. I broke up with him remember?"

"Yea but, " Kara begins then stops, contemplating her next words.

"We thought you guys would've made up by now," Blair says, stepping in. "We loved Max, the way he looked at you, the way you looked at him. I wish," she stops.

I ask, "You wish what?"

Kara answers, "We wish we had someone like that. He was perfect for you and…"

"You fucked it up," Blair finishes.

Well this is not what I expected.

"Well shit guys, thanks for trying to cheer me up!" I say and turn to leave.

"Wait Jade, we're sorry," Kara says, stopping me.

"Look Max and I are done. He's obviously moved on and so have I. Just leave it alone!" I order.

Their words sting. Were they right? Did I ruin things? Was I the problem? Was Damon my karma? It was all just too much to process. Blair remains silent watching my every move. I'm sure she is worried; she hasn't seen me this way in a very, very long time.

Concerned, she places her arm around my shoulders, "I think you need a night out with the girls."

I visibly cheer up, "You guys don't have to."

"Come on Jade, my treat. Honestly, Jayson has been driving me crazy the last few days and I could use some fun my damn self!"

Kara adds, "And when am I not having guy problems! I need a girl's night out!"

❧

"I'm only going out with my friends. Why is that a problem all of a sudden? You go out with yours," Blair whispers into her phone.

We're at my house getting ready. Kara and I share a silent "Jayson is a dick" exchange as Blair paces the living room trying to conceal her argument. Kara is seated at my vanity doing her makeup while I'm sitting on the floor curling my hair.

"Jayson, I'm not doing this with you right now! You go out with your friends and stay out all hours of the night and now you want to give me shit? Yea whatever." She stops trying to hide her frustration, "No you're not being fair. What's the big fucking deal? I'm not allowed to have friends? Umm hmm, well enjoy your fucking night!" She yells before hanging her phone up and tossing it onto the couch.

I look at my friend concerned. She didn't deserve to go through what she does. Sometimes I look at her and see my mother; a woman forced to dim her light because she chooses to be with a dark man. A little fun was definitely much needed for all of us.

"Are you ok Blair?" Kara asks.

"He's such an asshole!"

"You said a mouthful there girl," I mumble.

Kara nods in agreement, "Right! Aren't all men?"

We all giggle. Blair's mood noticeably improves and she joins us in my bedroom to finish getting ready.

"Y'all sure y'all want a man?" Blair jokes. "Having one isn't all it's cracked up to be."

"But being single isn't all it's cracked up to be either," Kara says.

❧

We finally make it to Viper. It is a super cute lounge nestled right in the center of Philadelphia. There were fire pits situated along the deck outside, which were lined with plush couches and tables.

"Wow you guys weren't lying! This place is nice!" I say.

We get situated at our table and order a round of drinks. The night is young and full of so many possibilities. By our second drink, we all calm our nerves forgetting all of our problems, even if it was only for the night. I was grateful to my friends for insisting that we have some fun. Damon and Max were far from my mind.

After spending some time at Viper, we're still ready to keep the party going. That's the thing I love about Center City, there are so many things to get into at any given moment. We settle on a small trendy restaurant for some dinner followed by the Smoke Lounge for some hookah and more drinks. By two a.m. we are still going at it. After kindly being asked to leave the bar because they were closing, we reluctantly call it a night and walk towards the parking garage to retrieve my car. Walking up the street, we pass what appears to be a little hole in the wall type of bar. To our surprise, we can hear the music still going and we are eager to check it out. Once we present our ID's to the bouncer, we make our way inside.

We enter the club and the music pumps, causing the walls to pulsate; the vibe is infectious. Making our way through the crowd, we notice that there are a lot of men. In fact, there's nothing but men throughout the entire space. Confused, we stop and look at each other. Kara mouths OH MY GOD and her eyes light up with excitement. Somehow, we made our way into a gay nightclub. The setting was perfect, the walls were black and the ceiling was high. The different colors from the strobe lights bounce off the walls and the crowd settled in the middle of the dancefloor.

The place was definitely rocking and there was no reason to leave. In fact, I'd prefer to spend a night dancing and being carefree. We get to be around a bunch of beautiful men, without having to deal with their nonsense, it was exactly what I needed. Feeling exhilarated, I reach for my girls and we head towards the nearest bar. After grabbing the bartender's attention, I lean in whispering my request in his ear.

Once he leaves, I turn to Kara and Blair. "Thanks for taking me out tonight ladies, I so needed this," I say pulling them into a hug.

"We got you boo," Kara says.

"Always!" Blair adds.

By this time, the bartender returns with six shots of Patron and some lime slices. He lines them up in front of us as I smile before handing him my card.

"Six shots? You're my girl Jade but you're trying to kill us!" Kara whines.

I laugh, "Loosen up! Let's have some fun and forget about guys for once!"

Enticed, we all grab one shot glass and a lime slice. Simultaneously we hold our glasses up.

"Cheers!" We yell out in unison.

We take our shots and toss them back. The liquor courses through my body and I get a warm tingly sensation. After we take our second round of shots I start to really feel it. Blair, who obviously was inebriated by this point, walks to the dance floor and we follow. The music was infectious; I close my eyes and allow my body to become one with it. By this time the DJ spins "Sorry" by Beyoncé and we all lose it. We sing along to the lyrics and stick our middle fingers in the air casting away our troubles.

Before I know it, I have an extreme urge to use the bathroom. I turn to the girls and tell them my plan. Kara who's dancing with a cute guy and Blair who's in her own world, follow me towards the back of the club where a large restroom sign illuminates. The liquor made me foggy, I had to squint and focus on where I was going. Pushing our way through the crowd I see a familiar face standing by the entrance to the bathroom. He looks tense and uncomfortable. His caramel skin, chiseled chin, I squint harder to help focus on his face; I know him. He doesn't see me, but he's looking for someone. *What the hell is he doing here?*

Before I can process what's going on. Someone brushes past me in a hurry, nearly causing me to lose my balance. He was younger, about twenty-two with a bright smile planted on his face. He rushes towards the bathroom, and walks right up to Damon. The two hug and share a passionate kiss.

Finally the realization of what's going on hits me. "That's Damon."

Blair says, "That's who?"

Without saying another word, I charge at them. Bewildered, Blair and Kara quickly trail behind me. Damon and his lover are so wrapped up in one another they don't even notice me standing there. Enraged, I reach for their shirts, pulling them apart. The two tear away from one another; the lover is baffled and Damon looks like he had seen a ghost.

With shock in his eyes he says, "Jade, why, what are you doing here."

I scream, "What am I doing here? What the fuck are you doing here Damon?"

"P…please let me explain," he stutters, looking at my friends and then back to me.

By this time, Kara and Blair caught up to me and quickly put two and two together. I just caught my first love kissing another man. I glare at him with confusion, hurt, and most of all rage. Anger and liquor are seeping through my pores. Damon slowly takes a step towards me, both hands up and pleading with his eyes. He reaches out to touch me and I smack his hand away.

"Explain? Explain? You want to explain why you're here kissing a fucking guy when you told me you were out of town on business?"

"David, what is all of this? Who are these people?" Lover-boy asks.

"Oh hell no!" I hear Kara yell out.

By now we are causing a scene. Partygoers were turning their heads to see what all the commotion was about.

I turn to Damon's acquaintance, "Who the fuck is David?"

"David is my man! Now who are you?" he glares, refusing to back down.

"Who am I? Who the hell are you?" I say stepping towards him.

"His boyfriend bitch!"

"Bitch? Who the fuck are you calling a bitch? You're the hoe ass bitch!" Blair retorts.

"Jade stop," Damon pleads.

His partner begins talking shit and Damon turns around telling him to calm down. When I hear him say,

"It's not what you think," to him I lose it. I jump on both of them swinging, punching, and kicking whatever I could. Before I know it, Damon is trying to hold me down and his lover lunges at me. Kara and Blair instinctively jump on him clawing and slapping away at his flesh. There we are, in the middle of a club, a gay club, acting like a bunch of damn fools. In an instant, club security swarms the five of us; pulling us all apart.

"Get the fuck off of me you piece of shit!" I scream as I try to wiggle myself free of the bouncer's hold.

9

The next morning I wake up to a blistering headache. I hear Blair sleeplessly breathing beside me. Trying to recollect what happened the night before, I use my elbows to slowly sit up right. When I do, my arms and back immediately ache with pain. I examine my surroundings and my eyes burn, the sun is just way too bright. Groggily, I roll out of bed and stand onto my feet. Blu is lying on the floor watching me with suspicion. Walking over to my windows, I stumble over my shoe. I quickly pick it up and see the heel is broken and I make no attempt to recall what caused the damage. Kara, who is sleeping in the living room, rolls over on the couch. I shake my head and try to keep my balance. Upon reaching the window and closing the curtains, I slowly begin to remember what occurred the night before.

Rubbing my temples, I realize I'm extremely hung over. In need of a quick remedy, I stagger into the kitchen and pull out two Advil pills from the cupboard. I go to the refrigerator and grab a bottle of water. Popping the pills in my mouth, I quickly sip my water and swallow in one large gulp. By now, Kara has managed to pull herself up off the couch to join me in the kitchen. She looks exactly how I feel: like crap. Her usually well-kept hair is wild and all over the place, one of her false eyelashes is hanging off her eyelid, and her lips are puffy and red.

"I need an aspirin or something," she manages to say as she takes a seat on one of the bar stools.

I giggle, all too familiar with the feeling. Then I reach into the fridge and grab another bottle of water before dispensing two painkillers into her hand and placing the water onto the counter. Without saying a word, she instantly pops the pills into her mouth, and swallows with no hesitation. I grab a box of crackers and take a seat beside her.

Kara looks at me, "So what the hell was that last night?"

"Girl," I simply say.

"So, he's gay?" she presses.

"It would appear so." I shrug, "Now I know why he had such great taste."

We giggle.

"No Jade, that's not funny!" Kara says.

"I know, but I have to laugh right now or else I'll lose it all over again."

"You'll be alright girl," Kara says, reassuringly rubbing my shoulder.

Blair comes out from the bedroom rubbing her eyes. Blu follows and I get up to pour him some water and feed him.

"Jade!"

I can sense her attitude, "What Blair?"

"Please answer your phone! It's been ringing nonstop. You couldn't hear it?" She asks.

Blair obviously rolled out of the wrong side of the bed.

"Honestly, I didn't even know where my phone was," I say as I reach and take it from her.

I unlock my phone and see about ten missed calls from Damon, in addition to twenty unanswered texts. My fury from last night suddenly resurfaces.

I suck my teeth and slam my phone onto the counter, "So now that lying asshole wants to talk to me? Now that I know his secret? What a fucking joke."

Blair takes a seat before she interjects, "Jade, please calm down."

"Calm down? How the fuck can I calm down right now? Damon is gay Blair! Gay! How would you feel if you saw Jayson kissing another guy? Would you be calm?"

"Jade, look I love you but, you kind of brought this on yourself," she shrugs.

Blair's reasoning was appalling. I quickly ask, "I did this to myself? What the fuck are you talking about?"

"Your expectations are just way too high. It's like you're never satisfied and sometimes you can be a bit shallow. I mean, you had a great guy and dumped him basically because you're selfish and unrealistic! I hate to say it but you hopped right on to Damon because of your ego. You hate the fact that the relationship didn't end on your terms. You knew you had no business getting back with him. Everything about you and Damon was good on paper and of course you fell in love with the idea of it. You were so caught up in the fantasy and the sick gratification of having it all that you missed the signs. Seriously, what guy that's attracted to you doesn't want to have sex? Sadly, what happened last night is your karma."

Hurt and shocked by her words I stare at her in disbelief, "So I deserved this? You of all people know what I've gone through with Damon," I retort.

Blair nods her head, "Exactly! And I knew it was a bad idea from the start."

I couldn't believe what I was hearing, "You're really going to throw it all in my face and say it's my fault?"

I study her, I was sure she would realize how ridiculous she sounded. But Blair refuses to budge.

Enraged, I say, "Fuck you Blair! You want to call me selfish? I'd rather be selfish than miserable with a man that ain't shit! If having standards keeps me from ending up like you, well then praise the Lord. I think it's funny that you always have so much to say about everyone else's relationships, yet you can't even get your man to come home at night."

Blair's eyes scorch and I know that I took things too far.

She says, "Well last time I checked, at least I can keep a man Jade, and he definitely ain't checking for dicks!"

"Guys stop it!" Kara orders.

Kara's pleas fall on deaf ears.

I yell, "No, get the hell out!"

Kara and Blair look at me stunned and offended by my request.

Blair rolls her eyes, "This is so typical of you, always running from your problems."

I could feel that my face was turning red; I was beginning to boil over.

Once again I order, "I want both of you out of my house right now!"

They quietly gather their things as I go into my bathroom and slam the door closed.

Monday morning arrives and Blair and I still haven't made up. I can count on one hand how many fights we've had, and this one was the absolute worst. Unfortunately, Kara became a casualty of our massive blow-up when I kicked them both out of my apartment and refused to return her calls. I don't know, I was just too hurt and embarrassed. Part of me suspected that Kara shared Blair's exact sentiments but never had the balls to say it to my face. So instead, I blocked everyone out; all I could manage to do is sleep, shower, and occasionally eat.

With everything that was going on, I couldn't even imagine leaving my apartment or going to work. I called my boss, made up an excuse that I came down with the flu and took the week off to hide from the world. My self-imposed seclusion definitely proved to be a challenge, because in addition to Kara, my sister and mother were calling me nonstop. By Thursday, I hear a knock at my door. Still unwilling to face reality, I try ignoring it but it doesn't cease. Finally, I reluctantly peel myself out of bed and get up to go answer it. When I open the door, I see my sister Aleena.

"What the fuck Jade? I've been worried sick! Why haven't you answered your phone? What the hell happened with you and mom?" Aleena fumes as soon as she lays her eyes on me.

Her pestering makes my head spin out of control.

"Aleena! Please, not right now," I say as I rub my temples.

"Well when Jade? You look like hell by the way."

"Are you coming in or not?" I snort.

She walks into my apartment and I warily close the door behind her. We take a seat on the couch.

She asks, "Aren't you going to offer me something to drink?"

"You know where the kitchen is, and you aren't handicapped."

"Damn! You are in a mood today aren't you?"

I shake my head, "What are you doing here Aleena?"

Aleena rolls her eyes, clearly annoyed with my attitude. "I had business in town. And since you've been dodging my calls I decided to drop in and check on you. So, what's up?"

"Nothing."

"Jade! It's me your sister, remember? I know you! Now what the hell is going on?"

"Didn't you talk to mom?"

She nods, "Yes, she told me how you completely flipped on her and dad."

"That's all she told you?" I ask.

"She also told me about your ridiculous theory. Seriously, you are both tripping! Dad wouldn't do that to mom again. I'm sure there's a logical explanation for it all," Aleena reasons.

"Aleena how can you say that? You're so naïve. Dad is definitely up to no good and mom deserves better!"

Aleena becomes irritated, "I'm not naïve, I give people the benefit of the doubt which is something you clearly aren't capable of doing. Marriages go through shit, and our parents definitely had their fair share of drama! But I don't think dad would simply throw it all away, they just celebrated their 30th anniversary. Doesn't that mean anything?"

"Whatever."

"Jade, who ever said love and relationships are perfect? Find a perfect relationship for me please I beg you! Nate and I have our issues, but that doesn't mean our love is doomed. Shit if what you say is true, and mom decides to work it out and stay it's actually none of your business."

I say nothing.

"You've had this damn attitude with dad for years. Will you please let it go? Yes, he was wrong for leaving us, and maybe I was too young to understand. But you and I both know dad has been a great father and has given his all to make up for his mistakes. Mom forgave him, why can't you?"

"I just don't trust that he won't pick up and leave again."

"Seriously, how can you live your life like this? You can't control everything. If something is going to happen it's going to happen and there is nothing you can do about it. The best thing you can do for yourself and your sanity is to live in the moment and enjoy it. You should try it; trust me you'll be a lot happier."

I shrug. I was beginning to question who the older sister in this relationship was.

"Anyway, what else is bothering you? I know that's not it, you're not that dramatic."

I shake my head, dismissing her inquiry.

"Jade, whatever it is just spit it out! I beg you; I did not drive all the way up here from D.C. to watch you sulk."

"I'm fine."

Aleena orders, "Jade! I swear I'll slap you! Spit it the hell out!"

"Do you think I'm shallow?"

I needed to know if what Blair said was true.

Aleena is confused by my question, "No, of course not."

I sigh, relieved. Maybe there was hope for me after all.

"But, I do think that your standards can be a bit ridiculous sometimes," she continues.

My shoulders sink, "Since when is having standards a bad thing?"

"It's not. But sometimes I think you have this idea that everyone and everything is supposed to be perfect, and it's just not the case. You have to be able to see past someone's imperfections at times; you have to be able to see past your own imperfections too. If you don't you'll never truly be satisfied or happy," Aleena explains.

I shrug, "I don't know. I guess seeing what mom and dad went through when we were younger really messed me up. Between the fighting and the separation, I remember spending so many nights listening to mom crying. I told myself I would never settle for less than I deserve like I thought she did."

"Well," she starts.

"Well what?"

"Is that why you ended things with Max? I know you told me the reason but it truly didn't make sense to me. To be honest, I've never seen you so open to a guy, like ever. I," she stops.

"You what?"

"I just knew he was the one for you, the one to finally get you to settle down and commit," Aleena admits.

I feel a lump form in my throat.

"Yea, I had Max and I fucked that up!" I can't hold back the tears any longer. "I pushed him away and now he has a new girlfriend," I confess with a sob, "And to top it all off, I ran into Damon. He's back in Philly by the way."

"It's ok Jade," my sister says, taking my hand.

I continue crying, "No, no it's not. Dad probably hates me. Max hates me. Blair hates me. And Damon is gay."

"Wait, Damon what?"

I tell her about everything that happened; every detail of us reconnecting, his inability to keep it up, the blow up at the club, and my fight with Blair. She looks at me with horror in her eyes and it makes me feel even worse. Without saying a word, she pulls me in for a tight hug and comforts me.

"You can't blame yourself for this Jade. He's the piece of shit that was lying living a double life."

I shake my head, "But if I wasn't so fucked up, I wouldn't have messed things up with the person I actually love. I'm so stupid."

"You're not stupid. You're human remember? We make mistakes," Aleena says. After a moment she asks, "You love Max?"

I nod my head and admit, "Yes, yes I do. As much as I have tried to fight it, I can't. I really miss him."

"Well get him back girl!"

"How?"

She says, "Apologize for one, and stop trying to be so tough all the time."

"But, he has a girlfriend."

"Girlfriend or not, you still owe him an apology for being an ass. And shit, you never know maybe getting some closure will help you both," Aleena explains.

I shrug, "I guess."

"But right now that's the least of your worries."

I'm confused, "What do you mean?"

"You need to go get tested Jade."

Her statement offends me, "Why would you say that Aleena? So you're telling that because Damon is gay he also has HIV?"

Now she was the one that was offended, "Are you seriously asking me that Jade?" She shakes her head then continues, "To answer your ridiculous question, no of course not. You two didn't use a condom, and with all the STD's being passed around today you just never know. I mean Damon clearly isn't that responsible if he's been lying to you. You really don't know what he has been up to; that has nothing to do with his sexual preference, asshole."

I have no rebuttal; Damon and I both were irresponsible that night. She is right; I had to get tested.

Aleena stays with me for the rest of the evening, desperate to cheer me up. We watch our favorite movies including *Mean Girls* and *Vickie Cristina Barcelona*, order some Pho and share a bottle of wine. By the morning, I wake up and call my gynecologist right away. Luckily, I'm able to book an appointment later that afternoon.

"You sure you don't want me to come with you?"

"Yes, I'm sure. But thank you so much for being there for me."

We hug and she says, "You're my only sister that's my job."

We hug once more before she gets into her car and pulls away. Taking a deep breath, I get into mine and head to the doctor's office.

"Jade James!" The nurse says, entering the waiting room.

I instantly feel nauseous. Standing up, I quickly tuck my hair behind my ear and clutch my purse. With my head hanging low, I follow her to the examination room. I could feel my heart beating through my chest with each step. Once inside the room, the nurse motions for me to place my things on the free chair in the corner.

"My name is Alyssa," she smiles. "I'm going to take your weight and check your vitals to get started."

I peel off my shoes and step on the scale. It reads one hundred thirty five pounds. *Sheesh, I lost five pounds!* Next, Alyssa has me take a seat on the examination bed and she checks my heart rate and blood pressure.

She finishes up and writes down a few notes before looking at me with a smile, "Ok Jade, your heart rate and blood pressure look good. Now what can Dr. Goldstein help you with today?"

"Umm, I, I need to get tested."

She mindlessly writes down some more notes and orders me to undress from the waist down before handing me a medical gown. Once she leaves, I do as I'm told and slowly peel off my yoga pants and underwear. As I put on the gown, I feel like I'm wearing a scarlet letter on my forehead. Quietly, I take a seat back onto the bed and anxiously wait to see the doctor. A few minutes later I hear a soft knock on the door and my doctor appears.

Dr. Goldstein beams, "Hi Jade! How have you been?"

I try to smile.

"Uh oh. What's going on?"

I struggle to find the words. Although I want to be honest, I'm still too ashamed to tell her the entire truth.

"I reconnected with an ex and we were intimate. But I only recently discovered he's been having sex with other people," I explain.

She listens, nodding her head, "Do you know how many other partners he had?"

I shake my head no.

"And how often did you two use protection?"

"We only got physical once, but we didn't use a condom," I confess, ashamed.

"I see," she says.

"I know I was really stupid and irresponsible."

"We all make mistakes, I just hope that you will try and be more careful next time."

I nod my head in agreement. *She has no idea.*

"So, I think the best bet is to test for everything now and get it all out of the way. I'm going to have you lie back and place both of your feet up. I'll perform the HIV test last," she explains.

When she mentions HIV my heart nearly falls through my stomach. Dr. Goldstein washes her hands and puts on a pair of blue latex gloves. Then she takes a seat at the bottom of the examination table and gets to work. Once done, she asks me to put my clothes back on and exits the room. I stand to my feet and quickly redress. A few minutes later she re-enters.

"Ok Jade, I haven't detected anything that's abnormal. However, I've submitted your samples just to be sure," she says.

"Ok."

"We will call you with the results in a few days. Until then, please be careful and try not to stress yourself out!"

I sigh, "I'll try not to."

"I know relationships can get tough. But if you need to talk to someone, please let me know. I'd be happy to refer you to someone."

I smile, "Thank you Dr. Goldstein."

I walk out of the doctor's office feeling like a complete ass. It felt like my life was spiraling out of control. Not ready to go home and desperate for some clarity, I end up in a nearby park and take a seat on an empty bench. After going over our fight in my head for the hundredth time, I can't help but think that Blair was right; this all was my fault. Everything I've done up to this point led me here. Yes I was successful; I had the job, the place, the car. But I knew that I wanted more; I wanted someone to share it all with. Slowly, I come to terms with the fact that when it comes to love, I am my own worst enemy. My intolerance for anything less than perfection and the fear of getting hurt truly crippled me. I never really realized it until now. Funny how that works right? Before I know it, I'm up and walking into one of our favorite cafés. As soon as I walk in, I see Damon standing at the counter.

We lock eyes and my first instinct is to turn around and run. I can see his eyes are filled with apprehension, and sadness. But after a moment, he makes his way over to me.

"Can we talk?" Damon asks with caution.

I can't say that I blame him for being a bit scared to be in my presence. I mean I did try to claw his eyes out less than a week ago. I slowly nod my head yes and find an open table situated in the corner of the café. He goes back to the counter and orders two iced coffees before joining me and taking a seat. A few moments pass in silence. The barista greets us with our order and quickly places the coffees down. I suddenly realize how dry my mouth is and instantly take a sip of my drink.

Finally, I say, "Thank you for the coffee."

Damon smiles and relaxes a bit, "Jade, I want to tell you how sorry I am. Please believe me when I say that I never meant to hurt you."

"I appreciate that Damon, and I'm sorry too. It's just when I saw you, I lost it."

"Yea, I would've lost it too. Trust me I understand your reaction, I should've never lied to you," he says.

"How long has this been going on?"

He tenses up and I regret feeling the need to ask, but I desperately need to understand.

He sighs, "Since I moved to California. I met someone and it sort of just happened."

"So why did you want to reconnect with me?"

"You were my first love Jade, and I'm still very attracted to you. When I saw you, I realized that I couldn't go another ten years without seeing you again. Believe it or not, I really missed you; but I knew that I was still struggling with this. I was so selfish about it all," he confesses.

"You're saying all of this Damon, but I still can't help but feel confused by it," I say.

"I get that. I guess what I'm trying to say is that I miss you, I have feelings for you, but it's just not in a romantic way anymore. I value you as a person, and I value you as a friend. I mean we were friends before anything else right?"

"If you see me as a friend, why were you affectionate with me? Why did we have sex?"

Damon answers, "I didn't want to make you feel uncomfortable or like there's something wrong with you; because that's definitely not that case. That night I left your house was the first time in a long time that I got intimate with a female. I knew it was wrong and I shouldn't have let it go that far. Deep down, I knew the day would come when I would have to give you an explanation, but when that day presented itself I got scared."

I ask, "Was it anything that I did?"

"No of course not; I think I've been dealing with this my entire life."

"Does anyone else know?"

He swiftly shakes his head, "No, I keep thinking one day I'll snap out of it."

His revelation was shocking. I realize that Damon needed a friend, if nothing else.

I gently take his hand, "Damon, don't ever be ashamed of being you. You can't be honest with others if you can't even be honest with yourself."

"I'm trying Jade. What happened the other night really put things into perspective for me."

I snort, "You're not the only one."

"I hope that we can be friends after this," he genuinely says.

The idea of it sounds nice. I smile, "Maybe one day, I just need some time."

"I understand. If you ever need me, know that I'm here."

We both stand and hug. After what felt like an eternity, I finally let it all go.

10

Later that evening, I receive an urgent call from my mother asking me to come by. When I ask her what was going on, she only insists that I be there by eight o'clock. As I pull into my parent's driveway, I notice my sister's car was there as well. I instantly feel nauseous, this must be it; my parents are going to break the news of their divorce. My mother must've decided she had enough of dad's cheating ways. Although I was proud of her for taking a stand, a part of me was sad that this all had to happen in the first place.

I can hear the sounds of the television as I sift through my keys and unlock the front door. To my surprise, the living room is empty. Suddenly, I can hear voices coming from the kitchen and quickly head in that direction. After a moment, I see my mother, father, sister, and another woman I've never met sharing a drink. They all see and greet me; I was confused because they were all…happy.

"About time you got here!" Aleena says.

My mother beams, "Jade! Hey baby."

She approaches me and pulls me in for a warm hug. Then, my father stands and joins us, giving me a hug before handing me a wine glass.

"Tracy, this is our oldest daughter Jade. Jade, this is Tracy," my father announces.

Tracy stands and greets me with a handshake, "Nice to finally meet you Jade."

By now I'm completely perplexed. If my memory served me correctly, this is the same woman I caught calling my dad, the woman my mother suspected was having an affair with my father. And here she was, shaking my hand like shit was cool.

I can't take it anymore, "Can someone please tell me what's going on?"

My mother chuckles and then fills my glass with wine, "Well now that you're here, let's all go into the other room and have a seat."

After what seems like forever, we are all seated in the living room. I take a sip of my wine and nervously bite my bottom lip, I feel like I'm about to lose it.

Finally, my father breaks the ice, "Jade, Aleena, the reason your mother and I invited you over tonight is that we have some important news to share with you both."

"You're getting a divorce?" The words leave my mouth much faster than I'd like.

I feel Aleena pinch me on my thigh; I know it was her way of telling me to shut the hell up.

My dad gives me a stern look, "Jade you're mother and I are doing just fine. I'm not having an affair and we aren't getting a divorce. Can I finish making my announcement now?"

I nod my head and keep my mouth shut.

"Now, as I was saying. Over the last two years, I've been taking some money and making some private investments. This is why I've been working so many hours. Tracy here is the niece of a good friend of mine, she's into all that technology like all you damn kids today and she created one of those apps you download on your phone. I agreed to be a silent partner and foot the bills using my savings and retirement for a percentage of the company. Now, I kept it a secret from you all and your mother because I knew y'all would try to talk me out of it. And when Jade got her mother thinking I was cheating, she dropped in on one of me and Tracy's important business meetings."

I shoot a quick look at my mother, who's smiling from ear to ear.

My father continues, "Well last week, all of Tracy's hard work paid off because the app was purchased by a big player in the tech industry."

"Wait, what?" Aleena says what we were both thinking.

"Your dad and I just hit the jackpot," Tracy elaborates.

I'm still suspicious, "What app is this that you created?" I quickly pull out my phone and go to Google.

Tracy explains, "GymClique. It's an app for people to find workout partners or groups in their area. It officially launched almost a year ago and it's currently the top fitness app out."

The name sounds familiar. I quickly type it into my browser and click search. Once I do, I see that everything my father and Tracy said were true. In an instant, I'm overcome with a sense of relief and excitement.

"It's true," I say.

My father stands up, "That's right! I've made back all the money I've invested plus a lot more. All because I took a bet on a young girl with big dreams!" He says as he places his hand on Tracy's shoulder. "With that being said, you're mother and I have decided to retire early and travel for a while. We will need you both to check on the house from time to time while we're away."

"Congratulations Dad! You deserve to relax and see the world." Aleena says before standing up to hug both of my parents.

I follow suit and say, "I'm so sorry dad. I should've never accused you of anything like that. I'm so proud of you, you and mom deserve it."

He kisses me on my forehead like he used to do when I was little, "You all are my world, and I would never do that to you again. Your mother is it for me; I was just young and dumb. It wasn't always perfect, but what is?"

I smile and nod in agreement. Out of the corner of my eye I see Tracy and my mom talking and I decide to join them.

"Tracy, I'm sorry about what happened the last time we spoke."

"No worries Jade, I probably would've done the same thing," she smiles.

"Thank you for helping my father out."

"No, thank you for having such a great father. You and Aleena are the reason he even took a chance on me and my dream."

"Why is that?"

"He said that my drive reminded him of you both."

I feel tears form in my eyes.

"Let's make a toast!" My mother cheers.

We all raise our glasses and toast to new beginnings.

I wake up the next morning feeling better than I had in days. My improved mood was like a second wind; giving me to energy to take care of the things like going to the gym, responding to unanswered emails, and cleaning my apartment. All of which were tasks that I neglected earlier in the week. By the time I finish getting my life back in order, I realize how much I miss my friends. Not being able to call them and tell them about my run-in with Damon or to share my parent's exciting news hurt like hell. Deep down, I hated the way things went south; and I knew a lot of it was my fault. At that moment, I understood that in order to move forward, I needed to start taking accountability for my actions. How can I hold everyone around me to such high standards and asking for perfection when I'm so flawed myself?

I knew that in order to make amends, I would have to call Kara first. Kara hated confrontation and was much more forgiving than Blair. I quickly pull out my phone and dial her number. She answers on the third ring.

"Hello?"

I knew that it was best to jump right in, "Hi Kara. I'm sorry that I've been dodging your calls. I just needed some time, do you forgive me?"

I can hear her smile through the phone, "Of course. I get it; we all know how Blair can be. You both are hard-headed it you ask me."

Once we smooth things over, she tells me that she and Blair made plans to go to brunch later that afternoon and insists that I join them. Much like me, she was ready to put everything behind us and move forward as friends. I beg her not to tell Blair, I was scared that she wouldn't show if she knew I would be coming.

I arrive at Honey's a few hours later. It was one of our favorite places to come for brunch and girl's talk. We've spent many weekends in this place, supporting each other through all of our trials and tribulations over the likes of French toast and coffee. I was hoping the nostalgic location would assist with helping us bury the hatchet. When I walk through the doors, I instantly spot Kara and Blair sitting in a corner towards the back. Kara can see me coming, but Blair's back is facing me. I quietly reach their table and smile, a timid indication of my succumbing.

"Well hello," Kara says with a grin.

Blair quickly looks back at me and I can tell she's still pissed.

She rolls her eyes, "What's she doing here?"

Kara says, "Blair cut it out. We're all friends; she's here to patch things up. This mess has gone on for too long if you ask me."

"You sure you're not here to start more shit?" Blair looks at me and snorts.

I shake my head and raise my hands in surrender, "No not even close."

She stays silent, waiting to hear what I have to say next. Kara motions for me to sit and I quickly take a seat in the free chair beside her.

"I'm so sorry guys. I should've never come at either of you like that and disrespected you. I know now that you both were trying to be a friend to me. I think I was so caught up in my problems I resorted to victimizing myself and not seeing the error in my ways. I realize I do have some issues, which I'm working on." I can feel my eyes swell with tears, "I really miss you guys."

An upbeat waitress approaches our table and places three waters down, "Hi ladies are you ready to order?"

Blair smiles and quickly answers her, "We only need another minute thank you."

The waitress returns the smile, "No problem, let me know if you have any questions."

We all thank her as she turns and walks away to tend to her other tables.

Blair takes a long sip of her water and places it down, "I miss you too Jade. And I'm sorry for the horrible things I said to you. I shouldn't have said anything."

"You're my best friend, I appreciate your opinion. Yea you can be a little tough with your delivery at times, but I know there wasn't any malice behind it. You were right; I can be selfish and relentless with my expectations. What happened with Damon was the wakeup call that I needed. I just wasn't ready to accept that at the time."

Blair nods, her demeanor softening, "I understand."

Kara claps, "Thank you! Now can we finally hug this out and get something to eat? I am starving!"

We all giggle and stand to hug one another. The waitress returns and we quickly get back into our seats and scan the menu. Once we place our orders, we spend the rest of our time catching up. I waste no time giving them all the details of my last encounter with Damon.

"Wait so you ran into Damon again?" Blair asks.

I quickly nod, "Yes! I went into our favorite coffee shop; you know the one on Broad Street? And there he was."

Kara almost loses her cool, "Girl! What happened? Tell us everything!"

It's been a few weeks since my friends and I made up and I couldn't be happier. Summer is officially coming to an end. I'm always amazed at how quickly time passes by. The last few months have been a whirlwind of experiences;

a lot of ups, and plenty of downs. But when an old season ends, a new one begins with new opportunities and lessons to be learned, and I was ready for it. Blowing my chances with Max, finding out my first love was gay, falling out with my parents and my best friends put a lot of things into perspective for me. Being vulnerable no longer scared me. It wasn't easy to admit, but I'm far from perfect and I like it. Life isn't meant to be perfect, love isn't meant to be perfect, relationships aren't meant to be perfect; there are times when you have to take the good with the bad. And as long as I stay true to my values and myself, I'll be ok. Knowing this now, I am able to breathe a little easier and to take unnecessary pressure off of myself. Instead of stressing about getting my happy ending before I hit the tender age of thirty, I'm determined to enjoy the ride as I go. I don't care what anyone says; I had a hell of a run in my twenties. I accomplished a lot, I learned a bunch, and I feel as fabulous as ever!

In true fashion, I dress cheeringly, anxious to have a great night with my friends and just celebrate life. It felt like it had been ages since I've had carefree fun with the ones I loved. It's Blair's thirtieth birthday and I wouldn't miss it for the world.

I put a few intricate curls in my hair and finger-comb them to create easy loose waves. Aiming for a simple and effortless look, I reach for my crimson lipstick and fill in my lips. The red was a boost of color to my white jumpsuit; a prized find that was sleeveless and open in the back, the wide legs complimenting my long silhouette. Once I put on my favorite strappy heels I take one last look in the mirror and am satisfied with my appearance. Adamant to being on-time, I grab my clutch and gift before dashing out the door.

At the party, I navigate through the building entrance and am highly impressed. Blair wasn't kidding when she said she was doing it up big for her birthday this year. The venue itself is breathtaking. This place was popular among hip business-people; the rooftop lounge offered a million-dollar view of the city. The elevator ride is comfortable on the way to the top floor.

Once I step off the elevator, a doorman greets me with a smile, "Are you here with a party?"

I return the smile and nod yes, "Jade James for Blair Montgomery."

The cute doorman quickly scans the list and nods his head once he locates my name.

He takes my left arm, "Nice watch."

"Thanks!" I say as he secures my silver wristband.

I enter the lounge and see a bunch of familiar faces. Navigating through the crowd, I say hello to all that I knew. There is a roped off area with a bunch of balloons and I know that is Blair's section. I quickly make my way over there and show my wristband to stocky bouncer to gain access.

Blair spots me and yells out, "Jade! You're on time!"

I giggle and she runs over.

I happily greet her holding a bouquet of lilies and a small gift bag from Tiffany's, "Happy birthday!"

Her eyes light up with excitement and she hugs me, "Oh my goodness! Thank you Jade!"

Blair looks amazing; her hair is slicked back into a straight ponytail that barely touches her butt. Her makeup is done to perfection. She's wearing a silver glittery romper that accentuates her curves and compliments her chocolate skin. All eyes were definitely on her.

Kara makes her way over to us. "Yes Jade, you look bomb.com!"

We all giggle.

I shake my head, "No girl that's you! And birthday girl over here!"

Kara replies, "Don't she? Ms. Blair is ready for her thirties girl, she played no games!"

"You're damn right! It's my night!" Blair agrees.

Blair grabs our hands and drags us to the private bar set-up in her area. She quickly pours three glasses of champagne and hands them to us.

We raise our glasses and I say, "Here's to Blair, thank you for being you. I love you and I wish you nothing but happiness as you venture into this new chapter in your life."

Her eyes water, "Aw! I love you too!"

Before we tap glasses and take a sip Kara interrupts, "Wait! I want to make a toast too! Here is to love, friendship, and being even more fabulous in our thirties!"

Blair says, "Well, I guess I should add something too. Here is to always being true to ourselves and never forgetting to love ourselves first."

Finally, we hold our glasses up and toast. After taking a sip, we're more than ready to party; and that's exactly what we do. Not long after, Jayson approaches us and Blair is whisked away. With her man on her arm, she works the room like royalty; when you're the lady of the hour, your presence is in high demand. Kara and I let her do her thing as we get another drink and hang by the bar. I'm thankful because lately I've been so focused on working and getting my shit together I neglected to check in on my friend and see how she was doing.

"So how are you Kara?" I ask.

She forces a smile, "I'm good. You know, can't complain."

Almost immediately I know something is wrong, "You sure?"

She looks to the floor, fixes her fuchsia dress and sighs, "I'm sure you're tired of hearing about my relationship problems."

"Whether I'm tired of it or not, I'm still your friend," I pause, waiting for her to make eye contact. When she finally does, I finish, "I'm here for you."

Kara smiles, "Thanks Jade."

She tells me about Rashad ditching her tonight, making up some bogus excuse about being sick. As she finishes her story, an old college buddy of mine interrupts us. We spend the next few minutes catching up and exchanging numbers. Suddenly, I see a familiar face across the room. His brown skin, strong jaw-line, and jet-black hair looked more pronounced than I can remember. Memories of us and our time together rush back to me like the floodgates, causing my skin to grow hot. My stomach turns as I long to be back in his arms, and to feel his lips on mine. Before I know it, I excuse myself and am walking towards him; drawn to him like a moth to a flame. I approach him; his back is now turned towards me as he is engaged in a light conversation with a female, another admirer I suppose. I reach out and softly tap him on his shoulder. He turns around and his demeanor changes, causing me to instantly regret coming over.

"Hello Max," I muster up the courage to say.

Behind him, I can see his acquaintance excuse herself. The music loudly pumps through the crowd, but I swear that I can hear my heart racing. After what feels like an eternity, he leans in and kisses me on the cheek.

"It's good to see you Jade," he coolly replies.

I say, "Crazy seeing you here."

"I ran into Blair the other day, she invited me."

He sips his drink and softly rocks his head to the music. I refuse to let my nerves get the best of me. I imagined this day for a long time, knowing that if I ever had the opportunity to see him again and that I would own up to all of my mistakes.

I take a moment and softly exhale.

"Listen Max, I want to apologize from the bottom of my heart. I'm so sorry for screwing things up. You were right about everything, I was scared and I never realized it or even wanted to admit that to you. I didn't understand how wrong I've been for so long. I know I'm asking for a lot, but if you can find it in your heart to forgive me and just, I don't know be my friend. I miss you Max," I can feel my eyes swell with tears as I pour my heart out.

Max stays silent, almost too silent. I swore that if he didn't say something soon that I'd be forced to bolt out of that place and run for cover.

But finally he says, "I told you that I don't need any more friends Jade."

My heart sinks into my stomach. It was foolish of me to think things would be ok just like that; I really blew things with this guy. I had to get out of there before I embarrassed myself any further.

I struggle to find my voice, "I understand. I hope you enjoy the rest of your evening."

I quickly turn on my heels and fight back my tears.

Suddenly, I feel his hand grab mine, "You didn't let me finish. I can't be friends with you Jade, not if I can't be with you. I miss you too. I love you Jade."

My head spins with relief; it all seemed like a dream. "You do?"

He chuckles, "Of course I do. You're the one that dumped me remember?"

I shamefully nod my head and pull him in for a hug, so ashamed of some of my stupid and rash decisions. I can't help myself; I need to be in his arms again. He hugs me back and I melt, lost in the moment. But too soon I quickly remember the girl I saw him with at the mall.

I pull away, "Wait, don't you have a girlfriend?"

He laughs again, "Oh you're talking about the one you saw me with at the mall? Blair told me that you guys saw us."

I quickly nod. I missed him but I wasn't in the business of stealing other people's men, no matter how badly I wanted him for myself.

"That didn't work out," he explains.

"Why not?"

He looks into my eyes, all jokes aside and says, "She wasn't you."

BLAIR

I take a sip of my champagne and can't help but smile. I scan the room and see that everyone is having a great time. The music was rocking, everyone was dancing, and the weather was amazing. This night was turning out to be perfect. I was thankful to have some many great people in my life and the fact that they were all here for me meant a lot.

I see Jade and Max talking and my heart skips with anxiety. *Goodness I hope they can work it out!* I love Jade to death but sometimes I feel she can be her own worst enemy with her stubbornness. So when I randomly bumped into Max a few days ago, I couldn't help but convince him to come to my party. When I see them hug and kiss and I want to do cartwheels! *FINALLY!* I knew they were a perfect match from the moment I met Max, I'm glad Jade finally realized it also. Now in addition to my birthday, there's even more reason to celebrate. I turn and head to the bar ready to order some shots and toast to their reconciliation.

As I make my way there, I pass the door to the hallway leading to an empty stairwell. I instantly notice Jayson; he's preoccupied in what appears to be a deep conversation.

His arms are crossed, his face is tense and I can literally see the steam rolling off of his skin. The music is too loud; I can't see who he's talking to or what he's saying. All that I can make out is that he is angry, very angry. The last thing I want is for him to be in a sour mood, because essentially that will ruin my night and that absolutely cannot happen! I make my way over but he doesn't notice me. Finally, I am close enough to hear them.

Jayson orders, "You need to leave."

"No! I'm sick of this shit," she says.

"Look, don't cause a scene. I'll hit you up later on. Please go home Renee," he insists.

Instantly I get sick to my stomach. This isn't the type of conversation I expected to walk in on. A familiar sense of humiliation takes over me but I resign to wait and listen; refusing to jump to conclusions. I make sure I'm hidden well enough behind the door so that they don't see me.

"Jayson, you need to tell her right now or I swear I will walk out there and say something. You know I work here why the fuck would you let her have a party here? Do you know how that feels to know you're here with her?"

Now my skin is burning.

"She's my girlfriend why are you tripping it's not like I did this shit on purpose."

"I don't give a fuck if she's your girlfriend! I'm the one carrying your fucking child!"

Their conversation and the music make my ears ring. I stand there paralyzed. Her words playing over and over again in my head like a broken record. My head is spinning and the realization of what I just heard makes me nauseous. Before I know it, I'm covering my mouth and running in the opposite direction towards the bathroom.

46345059R00094

Made in the USA
Middletown, DE
29 July 2017